Helen and Desire

Helen and Desire

Alexander Trocchi

Introduction by Edwin Morgan

This edition first published in Great Britain
in 1997 by Rebel Inc.,
an imprint of Canongate Books Ltd,
14 High Street, Edinburgh EH1 1TE

10 9 8 7 6 5 4 3 2

British Library Cataloguing in Publication Data

A catalogue record for this book is available on
request from the British Library

ISBN 0 86241 629 9

Typeset by Palimpsest Book Production Limited,
Polmont, Stirlingshire
Printed and bound in Finland by WSOY

Introduction

EDWIN MORGAN

Alexander Trocchi's reputation always had elements of the problematic, though unease rather than opposition seems to have been the main factor, where doubts existed. Many of his works had an underground life only, and their non-respectability made them suspect, even though – or perhaps because – they sold well and were much reprinted and were translated into several languages. Even his 'accepted' novels, *Cain's Book* and *Young Adam*, whose quality and power of writing must be clear to any reader, were frequently out of print, or if in print, proved elusive in bookshops, whether through a sort of moral censorship by booksellers, a deliberate under-promotion by publishers, a timid public demand, or a mixture of the three. The result of all this was, in any case, that it was hard for any interested person to get a sense of Trocchi's *oeuvre*, and so to weigh its worth. The situation improved when Andrew Murray Scott brought out his biography (*Alexander Trocchi: The Making of the Monster*, Polygon, 1991) and selection of extracts (*Invisible Insurrection of a Million Minds: A Trocchi Reader*, Polygon, 1991), but the anthology still did not contain anything from the erotic novels, and missed an opportunity to help readers see if the links between underground Trocchi and overground Trocchi bring forward values that ask to be taken into account. In fact they do, and it is good to have the best of these books, *Helen and Desire*, first published by Olympia Press in Paris in January 1954, reprinted now.

The erotic novels Trocchi wrote in France in the 1950s were obviously a means of making money quickly, but they have also to be seen against the background of his work as editor of the magazine *Merlin* (1952–55), which published Beckett, Sartre, Genet, Henry Miller, Hikmet and Ionesco, and championed the exploring of alienated (Sartre) or forbidden (Genet) or absurd (Ionesco) experience. The first number included a critique of existentialism (by A.J. Ayer), and this philosophical marker, placing existence before essence, was to pervade Trocchi's fiction, where, as the narrator of *Cain's Book* says, a writer should 'annihilate prescriptions of all past form in his own soul' and should judge what he writes 'solely in terms of his living'. This must involve not only subject-matter but also language. In the joint introduction to *Writers in Revolt*, an anthology co-edited by Trocchi, Richard Seaver, and Terry Southern (1963), we are told:

> The exploratory nature of art should be welcomed, for it may reveal an answer. But while we have grown conditioned to accepting implicitly, and welcoming, each new advance or discovery in medicine or science – or now in space research – limiting our reservations, if any, not to the scientist's methods or even his ends, but at most to the applications, the writer still struggles for the freedom to use his tools – language – without restrictions ... What is required, then, is the deliberate avoidance of lip service to assumed values, and adherence instead to deeply personal impulse, as well as the active response to the most private value inclinations.

The exploring, the deconditioning, the freeing, the transvaluing are seen in the outsider heroes of *Cain's Book* and *Young Adam*, but equally in the outsider heroines of erotic novels like *Helen and Desire* and *Thongs*, published under the female pseudonyms of Frances Lengel and Carmencita de las Lunas. And just as the first-person narrator of *Cain's Book* is shown as actually writing that novel through the course of the action, so too the first-person narrator of *Helen and Desire* is shown writing her own story. Joe Necchi types his novel on a scow in New York harbour, and Helen Smith scribbles hers with a pencil in an Algerian tent or room, but in each case we are given a strikingly immediate insight into the mind and feelings of the existential exile. Doubtless Trocchi became ventriloquially female in order to satisfy the assumed demands of the male readers of erotica, but he obviously relished the challenge of the transformation and entered into it with zest and thoroughness. In addition, he uses the sexuality of his heroine, in those proto-feminist days of the early 1950s, to establish a formidable presence: not only a beautiful, fair-haired, physically strong young woman who can make the 'editor' of her story exclaim, 'What a superb creature she must have been!' but something much more interesting, being on the one hand a boldly inventive and intelligent wordsmith and on the other hand an almost primal embodiment of sensuality, the very incarnation of desire as the book's title suggests, a desire that is virtually Lacanian in its insatiability, its identification with her existence.

Beginning as an adolescent loner in an Australian village, rejecting the received ideas and expectations of a narrow, restrictive, parochial society, she is ripe for escape, travel, adventure, exile, her quick-witted and often ruthless sense of self-preservation making her the natural heroine of a picaresque novel, where the action moves from Australia to Singapore to India to France and finally to Algeria. The lushly described sexual encounters, with both men and women, which punctuate the book are of course the *raison d'être* of an underground publication and yet are also one of the means Trocchi uses to transcend the genre. On an obvious level, which must strike any reader, there is the fact that Trocchi hardly ever employs the so-called taboo words which a novelist today would freely indulge in; the language is positively baroque, even to the borders of parody (Trocchi's wit can sometimes be seen behind Helen's, dropping a sly over-the-topness – just a pinch! – into the *olla podrida*), and has a recurring kinaesthetic strangeness as Helen gropes for verbalisation of the sensations her whole flesh seems designed to receive. The imagery is memorable. 'The lilac putty of my nipples was as heavy and ambiguous as mercury.' 'The cutting shingles . . . crackled like china chips.' 'My glistening torso slithered under discs, flats and surfaces, under flanges of containment and protrusion.' 'His white skin gleamed moistly, like a mushroom in moonlight.' 'We had writhed on soft gimbals . . . gliding on soft graphite, passing and repassing.' 'The hairs of his chest were like live terminals against the amorphous sludge of my breasts.' 'The shifts, the slips, the slides, the slithers, the glides, the rolls did not move so much as concentrate a stranded passion.' 'The seed, as incandescent as magnesium, in my loins.' 'In the lonely meadow of her bed.'

But Helen is more than a stylist. As she sits in her Arab tent in Chapter 2, a sexual prisoner, well fed, solitary yet available to all, thinking of her last anonymous partner, she meditates on the apparent paradox of her existence, rejoicing in her separateness, her non-attachment, yet at the same time overwhelmed again and again by 'the terrible joy of annihilation, the deliverance of my whole being to the mystery of sensual union'. She writes because she is conscious of, and interested in, the paradox. She has, as a genuine existential hero, a story no one else can tell: 'I am anxious to record everything, to break through the shameful shell of civilised expression.' In another of her Algerian ruminations (Chapter 9) she finds a defence of oriental languor and passivity and subtle cultivation of pleasure against the western work-ethic which her Australian father, as a businessman, would have wanted her to believe in and (on his death) profit from:

> Everything is computed in terms of time, so much time for this, so much time for that; it must not be 'wasted'. Geared for industry, those stupid westerners never pause to analyse the word 'waste'. Time is accepted without questions as valuable; like money or land or food, it must not be 'wasted'; at the end of an hour one must have something to show for it. The question for them is: What 'excuse' for passing the hour in such and such a way? If one can produce riches at the end of the hour, then the time has not been 'wasted'. But if one has merely derived pleasure from living? If one considers living important – in itself?
>
> The western God, the Jewish God, was invented to make the hatred of life logical.

She sees the non-postponement of satisfactions as logical, even though she knows desire is infinite. We are reminded of what she wrote at the start of her travels in Chapter 2, after surrendering herself to a young man in the toilet of a train:

> As I slipped the dress back over my warm satisfied flesh, the true immensity of the adventure before me filled me with an ungovernable joy of living.

Could that teenage joy survive the extraordinary variety of her sexual encounters, with Ursula, with Duke, with Captain O'Reilly and his steward, with Chen, with Lieutenant Hawkes, with Abdullah, with Nadya, with Mario, with Devlin, with Youssef, and with the dozens of anonymous partners who filed through her flesh in the Algerian desert? Could it survive her own necessary deceits and manipulations as she struggled to outwit male oppression, male assumptions, male proprietorialities? Could it refuse to be sentimentalised by the unexpected and non-physical kindness of her only good angel, the wealthy Indian Parsee, Mr Pamandari? In her latter stages, as she is being fattened and lightly drugged on a diet of honey, almonds, and hashish by her Arab captors, she retains her clarity of mind (e.g. her wish to be revenged on Sheikh Youssef) but tries to describe how she is torn between 'the terrible pleasure I experience in approaching the unconscious state of an object' and the still unquenched desire to record what is happening to her. She almost argues herself out of her writing obsession: it's a bore, stupid, a 'ridiculous waste of time that might otherwise be *lived*'. But no, that won't do. Trocchi inhabits her. 'I think I write because it is a triumph. I feel the need to express that triumph.' Her manuscript ends in mid-sentence, and we never find out what happens to her, but if her last musings are valedictory, they are eloquently so:

> What am I doing still wielding this pencil? It seems to have stuck to my fingers. I can't get rid of it. Shores of experience slide away from me. The sky will be red tonight from my slit of a window. The roof-tops and the minaret at sunset will glow softly and noises of beasts and men and perhaps music will drift up to me before – after, oh yes after my beloved potion! – the door opens for another time and with a rising of my juices a male spine drives me to delirium.

It is a kind of defiance. The reader is not allowed to switch into a lulled mode of orientalism, with sunset minaret and street music; it is the fever of hashish and anonymous sex which lies in wait, and Helen is ready to ride the fever as it rides her.

Edwin Morgan
Glasgow, 1997

A Note on the Text

Helen and Desire has been abducted and abused more often than the heroine herself. Trocchi's best and most successful 'dirty book' has frequently fallen victim to pirate publishers or to the sharp practices of legitimate publishers who didn't honour their contracts, where they existed, with the author. Needless to say the text itself has undergone many minor, and some not so minor, changes during this existence in the hinterland of pornographic publishing. This makes fixing on a definitive text somewhat difficult.

Immediately successful on its first printing by the Paris-based Olympia Press in early 1954 (#2 in the Atlantic Library series), under the pseudonym of 'Frances Lengel', it was reprinted later the same year, again in 1956, and in 1962 appeared retitled as *Desire and Helen* in order to foil the unwanted attentions of the French vice squad.

Helen and Desire finally appeared under Trocchi's name from Brandon House, California, in 1967, and again in an Olympia edition, now based in London, in 1971. This edition, incidentally, qualifies for an award for the tackiest book cover ever. The novel *had* appeared in the United States even earlier, published by Castle Books of New York as *Angela* by 'Jean Blanche'. Understandably annoyed by this pirating, Trocchi secured a promise not to reissue this edition, but on the condition that he provided Castle with a 'new' *Angela*. This he did, retaining from the original only

Helen's upbringing, dispensing with the performance of writing her memoirs, and confining the rather dull story entirely to an Australian setting. *Angela* appeared in Britain in 1968 from Tandem Books.

As recently as 1991 a certain American publisher issued an unauthorised new version with the original narrative 'improved' by the addition of extra sex secenes, some so graphic that even Trocchi might blush.

As far as possible this *Rebel inc.* edition follows the original 1954 Olympia version. However, perhaps due to the haste with which Olypmia issued books, even that text is marred by a number of errors. Some of these have been corrected by comparison with later editions. In a couple of instances of doubtful syntax and punctuation the text has been corrected despite the lack of hard textual evidence to support these changes, but only in cases where all texts are deeply ambiguous to the point of confusion. The urge to tamper to any great extent has been resisted in order to preserve the full flavour of Trocchi's inimitable, if occasionally oblique, style.

John Pringle, 1997

COPY OF A LETTER SENT BY MAJOR PIERRE JAVET TO
HIS FRIEND, CAPTAIN JACQUES DECOEUR OF THE
FRENCH GARRISON AT MASCARA, ALGERIA.

Ghardaïa,
5 July 1949

Dear Jacques,

*Here is a pretty little thing indeed! You, who were always
going to be a writer, what do you make of it? Officially, of
course, no more than a routine enquiry. But for you! Could your
imagination have created such a woman? What a superb creature
she must have been!*

*The facts are as follows: the original manuscript, of which I
enclose a copy, was found on some stray Arab who was pulled
in here for theft. We don't quite know what to make of it. The
man says he found it. Of course, he's lying, but there isn't very
much we can do. We have a good idea as to the identity of the
sheikh mentioned in the manuscript. But again, we have to move
cautiously.*

*If anything breaks, I'll write you about it immediately. If the
woman is ever found – well, we shall see what we shall see!*

A bientôt,   *Pierre.*

Chapter One

It is dark where I am lying, alone, in a tent, on a few sheepskins that they provided for me. They have taken my clothes away from me and have given me the clothes of an Arab woman.

Outside, I can hear them speaking but I cannot understand their language. They are watering their camels. Soon I suppose someone will come in. But I am not really afraid. In the past I have always found that to be a woman is enough. I have only to wait. Some time we must reach a town where someone speaks English or French and then I will be able to explain. They will have to give me up. And then it may take a long time. But I shall plan. And I shall have my revenge.

How terrified I was when I saw the camels of Youssef's caravan move off in single file! And Youssef himself, the only living soul to whom I could speak, turning his eyes away as though I no longer existed!

One day I shall make him pay for all that.

Meanwhile I am going to go back to the beginning and write it all down – oh, I regret nothing! Not even this. Or what happened on the sand dunes a few hours ago. And Youssef, the poor fool, thought he was humiliating me! How like a man! I have met many men, and some of them have been fine strong beautiful men, but at bottom, I'm afraid, all men are fools.

It seems a long time ago now since I bathed in the coral-spined water in the little cove below our village. That was where life began for me, I suppose. It was, anyway, almost the beginning . . .

How difficult it is to explain! The terrible mute hunger in our bodies! If I touch my thigh here in the near-darkness of the tent my whole body is again instinct with the driving urge that brought me here, and I cannot explain it. As always, it is stronger than fear. For me it has always been that way. It is as though my whole history were contained in the touch, asserted again in the pressure of fingers, all my life laid out with the smooth curves of my body, maturer now, but young still, and waiting silently, yes, waiting, on these hard sunbaked sheepskins that they threw in after me. Oh, I could laugh! For I have only one feeling. I have only to touch the smooth slab of my thigh again and I feel triumphant!

And it was the same then, I suppose, as it is now. I was lonely. I climbed down over the rocks to the little cove.

In the northwest of Australia there is a long stretch of beach, wild and desolate, which gives on to the Coral Sea. This part of the Pacific is so called because of the vast pink stretches of coral reef which spread for hundreds of miles like pale wounds in the smooth turquoise shimmer of the sea. From the window of my room I could look out right across the sea shelf and the scores of coral were sometimes almost scarlet and sometimes, in the evening, almost black. Few boats came there except those of the fishermen of our own village, and most of them belonged to my father, who owned four boats and employed ten men.

The village itself was small and was situated high over the water and high over the little cove which, for a number of years,

I had regarded almost as my private property. I had swum there since I was twelve years of age and had seldom been disturbed. No stranger ever came there, only sometimes a courting couple from the village, but, as that sort of thing was severely looked upon, not often even the villagers.

By the time I was fifteen I had taken to going into the sea naked. That first time it was a sudden decision, no sooner thought than acted upon. The idea, for reasons which I was unable to analyse, seemed to explode through my entire body, becoming a sensation of weakness at my flanks and of excitement at my navel. I remember standing there at the edge of the water, my toes pressing into the sharp shingle, flexing the muscles of my calves and thighs, and looking for the first time downwards at the slim yellowish twist of my body. There, through the delicate hollow of my half-formed breasts, I glimpsed the beginning of a chevron of silky hairs, damp to the touch from the sweat of my young body, from which my long slender legs seemed to radiate like spokes. I realised then that in some mysterious way this was my body's centre, the axis of my desires, the mercurial fulcrum around which all my movements would henceforth pivot, and in whose ecstasy my female limbs, bared at that moment to the light sea wind, would find fulfilment.

Then, with my eyes closed, the victim of my sudden obsession, I moved like a sleepwalker into the sea which rose upwards over the finely haired skin of my legs until, with my knees submerged, the water became a circle of cool pain at each thigh. All the world was extinguished save for my own flesh and the softly pervasive flesh of the sea.

Gradually, I opened my knees and felt the hot centre of myself pulled downwards into the water as though by a gravitational pull, and, as the lip of the water swung coolly between my buttocks and took my lower belly within itself, all the tension in my body was released and I sank ecstatically backwards beneath the surface of the water.

How long I remained there, bobbing like a cork beneath the surface, I don't know. Every muscle and sinew was relaxed, so that my splayed limbs and the white curve of my torso in sinking were abandoned like flotsam to the relentless will of the water.

I count the sea my first love and, in a sense, the most immaculate, for there was no percussive sentiment between us to pollute the elemental tremors of our union; unlike the liaisons to which I later consented, the passion that fed it was an impersonal one.

When I came out of the sea I found I was bleeding. I must have gashed myself during my plunge on a sharp splinter of coral, for there was a small cut just above the knee on the sleek concave surface of my inner thigh. By the time I had waded ashore the blood, in twin streams, had trickled down as far as my ankle. I sat down on the shingle, drew my knees apart with my hands, and allowed the sun to strike the wound on which the blood had already begun to congeal.

My father, a narrowly religious man, forbade the hired hands to keep company with me. He viewed my approaching maturity with a mixture of fear and pride; fear, because among the menfolk in our village there was not one whom he would willingly have accepted as a son-in-law; pride, because, widower that he was, he found himself once again possessed of a desirable young woman who drew the glances of all the young men in the village. For my part, I despised the young men of the village, partly, I suppose, because of my father's constant admonitions, and partly because, having read widely from childhood of the world beyond the bleak sunstruck desert of the interior of Australia, I despised the mute fatalism of men who would live and die in an isolated village like ours. The world of the villagers led to abrupt limits on all sides. Although I had little opportunity for comparison, I knew intuitively that the men of our village had in some subtle way, doubtless because of the inflexible pressure of nonconformist religion, allowed their manhood to go from them. They were vulgar creatures and, like most vulgar creatures, suspicious and afraid.

This was probably the real reason why I avoided the beach where most of the village girls bathed. Although I would have been protected there by the strict conventions of the community, I was reluctant to exhibit the bold outline of my torso to the prurient eyes of the village men. I waited for the day when my father would be dead and I would be able to leave the village for the last time.

Such were my thoughts when, on the eve of my eighteenth birthday, I climbed once again down over the rocks to the isolated little cove below the village.

On the very next day I would be eighteen. I stood looking out far across the coral-studded sea for a long time, conscious again of the dull excitement at my roots that began the moment I decided to come there. For it was almost a ritual by this time. Without haste, I would remove my clothes until every shred of my being was exposed to the impersonal gaze of the sun and the sea. My lissome body, like a blade of grass in the light wind, exuded a pinprick sweat of excitement so that the slow surfaces of my belly and my flanks glistened like dull sequins in the sunlight. The hairs of my lower abdomen had spread by this time, and a tenuous filament of sleek hairs connected the strong jut of my mound to the deeply indented whorl of my navel. My breasts, grown hard with desire, were dully painful in their arched-up position, and the lilac putty of my nipples was as heavy and ambiguous as mercury.

As I came out of the sea, I moved my hands briskly against my limbs to remove the salt water which clung there. But I was unsatisfied. For the first time the sea had failed to bring relief to my limbs. In exasperation I threw myself down on the shingle and lay there on my front with my cheek pressed against the shells. I do not know what I expected other than to feel the thrust of the earth against me, perhaps nothing, for I was conscious only of the tension in my muscles and of the oblique sultering dilatation at my roots.

As I lay there, I caught sight of the log. It had been there for some days, washed in by the sea. It was half-rotten, fat, with a portion of the rough bark still intact. For a moment I looked only, and then, gradually, the knowledge of what I was about to do came over me like a sickness, the familiar weakness at my thighs, the hard little rotation of pleasure somewhere deep under my navel.

A moment later I was standing, looking down upon it, and then, sinking to my knees, I brought my sex close to the rough bark. My whole body quivered and, with a sob, I collapsed on top of it, crushing it against my crotch by the pressure of my knees, and against my breasts with all the force of my arms. So violent was the convulsion of my body that the log rose under me and my body toppled sideways, bringing the waterlogged weight of the wood directly on top of me, rough and damp, and bruising the delicate sun-dusky skin of the front of my torso. Meanwhile, my back and buttocks were ground against the cutting shingles which crackled like china chips as my buttocks, riven by an irresistible arrow of lust, tightened spasmodically to bring my flailing legs round the log to grip it with the force of a vice against the hungry jaws of my sex.

When the agitations of my body ceased, I lay quite still under the heavy hulk of the tree, and I opened my eyes and stared straight above me at the unchanging cobalt depth of sky that fell upwards into infinity without cloud and without horizon.

My body was painful from the superficial wounds which the weight and the rough texture of the tree trunk had inflicted upon me. I could feel the sting of broken skin at my knees, at the cleft in my thighs, and at my delicate breasts, but I could feel no hatred for the thing that had hurt me. Almost reluctantly, I moved from underneath it. The whole front of my body was red from its abrasive contact, and, here and there, the trickles of blood mingled with the muddy liquid which had exuded from the bark and with the green smears that were evidence that the tree had once been rooted in a fertile soil.

I returned to the sea to wash my wounds. The salt nipped them painfully and my clothes when I put them on chafed the tender skin. Soon, however, I was dressed and, without further thought for the pain, I turned to go home.

At that moment, the sound of a man's laughter came to me. For a moment I froze with fear. What if someone should have witnessed my actions? But then I realised that the laughter came from the far side of a line of rocks more than twenty yards away and that the rocks cut me off completely from the sight of whoever was there. I might have gone straight home then had I not heard a woman's voice call out in fear: 'No . . . please . . . I can't . . . let me go!'

Without further thought, I moved quickly towards the rocks. The panic in her voice excited me. Tired as my body was, it was aroused by the urgent secrecy in the woman's voice. My heart was beating fast as I scaled the rocks and brought my eyes to a level from which I could look down on them.

I saw them at once. They were lying close under the shade of a strangely shaped rock which was suspended over them like a stalactite, the woman – I recognised her as one of the village girls who had been in my class at school – with her skirt disarranged above her knees, a sharp crescent of plump white flesh apparent between the top of her stocking and the hem of the displaced skirt, and her face red with the struggle against the man – I did not recognise him at first – who was straddled on top of her, his arms pinioning hers to the ground. Occasionally, leaning the weight of his body on top of one of her arms, he released his grip with one hand, reached down, and clawed at the swelling white orb of one buttock which stuck out from the frilly lace of her knickers like the gleaming nob of a boiled egg from a tattered eggshell. But every time he did so, the girl bucked violently underneath him and he was forced to bring his hand back to her wrist again to prevent her escape. Suddenly, during one of these manoeuvres, the girl succeeded in toppling him over onto his side, and at once, before he had time to regain his balance, she had lifted a large pebble and struck him a glancing blow to his forehead. He uttered a cry of pain and brought his hands to his head while she, hesitating no longer, made good her escape. I watched her run quickly between the rocks and disappear from sight.

The man sat up, still rubbing his head, and at last I was able to recognise him. It was Tom Snaith, one of the young men of the village who had been to the war and who had returned when he was demobilised. As a matter of fact, he was employed by my father, who looked upon him as a blackguard and had threatened to fire him on more than one occasion. He was a dark-skinned young man of more than medium height, well-built, and he seldom appeared in public without a cigarette between his lips. Evidently he had decided not to give chase because now he lay back on the shingle and lit a cigarette. He held it in his right hand while his left, stretched out at ninety degrees to his body, lifted a heap of shingle and allowed it to trickle from his tilted palm back onto the ground.

I hesitated. An idea was beginning to dawn upon me. Snaith had at least been in the outside world. With his help I might be able to escape sooner than I had expected. Was that all that decided me? I don't know. I had seen him lying heavily on top of my schoolmate and my body, in spite of its cuts, was already eager to succumb again to the primal turbulence which I had lately experienced. I suppose I wanted him as well. I wanted him immediately. His heat hard as the tree had been, but warmer, and with more resilience. I had never seen a naked man.

Boldly, I climbed into view and walked towards where he was lying. He sat up quickly at my approach and I felt his eyes studying the nervous movement of my walk. When I was within speaking distance, he addressed me with a sneer.

'I thought your father told you not to speak to strange men?' he said.

'It was you who spoke,' I said.

'So it was!' he replied.

We looked at one another. And then I saw his eyes which, in his reclining position, were on a level with the hem of my skirt, move downward to my calves, which were almost gold from the sun, and remain there for a moment before he threw a glance upwards and said: 'Why don't you sit down?'

I did so without replying.

Suddenly he knitted his brows.

'How long have you been here?' he demanded.

I looked at him. He was wearing his shirt open at the neck, and the muscles of his chest were well-outlined beneath the dark hairs.

'Tell me something first,' I said. 'Why did you come back here – to the village, I mean?'

He threw his cigarette against the rock.

'God knows!' he said.

'Why don't you go away again?'

He laughed bitterly.

'It takes money,' he said.

'I could get money.'

'What do you mean?'

I noticed that his eyes had once again fallen to the small triangle of cloth where my skirt rucked up against my mound. I raised one of my knees, casually, but so that the white skirt fell away, leaving the heavy surface of one thigh exposed. For a moment he stared at the bare flesh and then he looked quickly at me.

'Together?'

I nodded. 'I can take the money from my father's safe,' I said.

'You mean it?'

'I was watching when you tried to make love to Peggy,' I said.

He grinned. And then suddenly his face relaxed and, as though he were making a tentative bargain, he laid one of his brown hands on the dull opaque skin of my thigh. A quiver ran through me. I was now beyond my own decision. I slithered on the shingle into a position such that his hand came into contact with the moist and tremulous hairs of my sex. A moment later, his shadow blotted out the world for me, his lips, slightly open, came against my own, and his hand moved upwards over the smooth skin of my belly, tracing a hundred contours of my thighs and buttocks, while I, losing the thread of all thought, arched my torso against him and waited for the inundation of relief.

Beyond the edges of myself, I existed at my lips, at the twin excitements high and hard beneath my shift against him, at the tip of the finger which, with slight pressure, broke the frail webs of sweat that my body exuded in its delirium, and fiercely at my woman's pole to where eventually his fingers came, opening like scissors inside me, flooding my virgin body with pain and pleasure until suddenly, my skirt high above my waist and the lower part of my torso abandoned to his will, his hard male core broke through between my cloven hair, and his angry movements culminated, his body rigid, in a javelin thrust that seemed to cleave me in half. The tension in my thighs relaxed. My outspread legs twitched nervously for a moment and then came to rest like long plant shoots on the shingle. The hard concentration that had existed in my flesh became liquid and the relief moved like a sensual lava through my limbs.

Snaith had opened the front of my blouse and his firm lips sucked voraciously at my left teat. The pliant flesh shaped itself to the ring of his mouth and I breathed more heavily again as, with the slickness of a camera shutter, a small needle of desire pricked through my loins. I moved my fingers through his dark hair, at the same time pressing the back of his head so that his face was almost buried in the fleshy part of my breast. Then, with my other hand between our bodies, I pressed against the flatness of his belly, downwards, mingling my fingers with the hairs of his crotch, until, his spirits reawakened by my caress, his buttocks tightened and his power moved again at the wet richness between my thighs. This time, one of his hands came round under my trembling buttocks and his middle finger slipped surely into the downy rut which ran like a gully between them. There, torso-thrust against torso-thrust and my plump golden thighs spread-eagled under the tufted white rectangle of his moving front, all the radiant juices of my young starved body mingled with the pearly male stream that marked the consummation of our union.

A few moments later, he drew away from me. I rolled over, bringing my thighs, which were hot and smeared with our love, together tightly as though to contain the strange male emission that I knew then for the first time. He meanwhile had rearranged his dress and was seated crosslegged smoking a cigarette. His first words were:

'Did you mean what you said?'

I was lying on my front, perfectly composed, my skirts decent once again, leaning on my elbows.

'We must go to Charleston,' I said. 'We can go south from there.'

'When?'

'Tonight,' I replied. 'Before my father takes the money to the bank.'

'And we can be married in Charleston,' he said, as though he were talking to himself. 'He won't be able to do anything then.'

Fortunately, he could not see my face. What a fool he was! The thought of marriage had never crossed my mind. To be a house-slave as my mother was, to lose my freedom and adapt myself to his absurd male requirements! That was my first experience of this kind of idiot male presumption – why do they assume that because we have need of their bodies we will be willing to submit ourselves to the drab pattern of their everyday existence? If a man is poor and must work, what an overbearing impertinence to expect a beautiful woman to harness herself to his venal and constricted existence! Such men should be housed in a stable after their toil, and, if it is a woman's pleasure, they should be loaned to her for her occasional enjoyment. I had to suppress the impulse to laugh in Snaith's face.

'We go tonight then,' I said. 'You must borrow a motorcycle and wait outside the house at midnight.'

He laughed.

'Don't worry,' he said. 'I'll be there.'

Chapter Two

I was not mistaken. I had just written those words that Snaith spoke to me when the heavy tent flap moved. I crammed the paper out of sight under the sheepskins. The man stood in shadow looking down at me where I lay.

For a few minutes he said nothing and then, suddenly, he pointed his finger at himself and said something which I could not understand. Perhaps he was telling me his name. When I did not answer, he continued to gaze down at me.

Under his impenetrable gaze, I felt something stir in me. It was as though some delicate plant inhabited my loins and was at that moment thrusting its roots and shoots into the darkest reaches of my flesh. I acted quickly, or rather, found myself acting quickly, for I did not consciously decide to play the part I did in the mute pantomime which followed. I was stripping myself of the robe they had given me. And then I was lying naked on my back in a prone position a few feet away from the man who looked down at me. My legs were heavy and apart. And then I was raising myself on my elbows, my body bristling in a tawny arch, my heels tight on the sand beyond the sheepskins, so that the hot halter of my loins rose like a snake about to strike at the man in the shadows.

For a moment he hesitated, and then, falling on his knees, he thrust his bearded face voraciously against my sex.

* * *

. . . Once again I have experienced the terrible joy of annihilation, the deliverance of my whole being to the mystery of sensual union, and this time with a male whom I would not recognise in daylight. There is perfection in that. I want nothing more of him. I rejoice again in my separateness, in the vital isolation that makes it possible for a human being to collide, to coalesce, and for a short while to coexist with another. That is the essence of it. I am not like those weak women who want to be owned by a man, body and soul, and who, having submitted to such an indignity, seek in retaliation to hedge him in, to have him belong – what would I do with a man for twenty-four hours in a day, for seven days in a week, and for months, years? That is a kind of slow poison. My life is my own. That is a truism. But in saying it I assert the fact that I am not like those women, devitalized by convention, who will mutilate their own personalities because they will not accept the fact that all great lust is impersonal, a drive in the very mineral part of us whose gleaming ore can only be tarnished by sentiment.

My limbs are at rest. The man is gone, as quietly and obliquely as he came. I do not suppose I will be disturbed at least until dawn. I am anxious to record everything, to break through the shameful shell of civilised expression and to penetrate into the pulsing recesses of my primal being. I want to have what I want to say said before they discover, and perhaps destroy, my record.

We arrived in Charleston about ten o'clock in the morning of my eighteenth birthday on a motorcycle which Snaith had stolen from the local blacksmith. We were tired and dusty after our long ride. We had stopped only once, at a truckdrivers' rest on the road. There we drank tea. Snaith fingered me under the table but I made him desist because I was anxious to get to Charleston as quickly as possible. I feared that my father might already have discovered our flight.

I had told Snaith that I had stolen fifty pounds. That seemed a fortune to him anyway. I lied because I felt sure he would ask me to hand over the money to him. He did so, almost as soon as we were on the road. I could hardly refuse him, but I congratulated myself on my foresight, for there was another two hundred pounds carefully fastened between my breasts under my chemise. I had no desire to be dependent upon Snaith.

We drew to the kerb in the mainstreet and, parking the motorcycle, we entered a restaurant. We sat upstairs near the window overlooking the street, and from where I sat I could see the motorcycle resting on the kerb. We ate breakfast and discussed our plans. It was Snaith's opinion that we didn't need to go any farther. We could be married there. I could write and tell my father and then, if everything went well, we could both return to the village and discuss the future with him. We could do worse, in Snaith's opinion, than to settle down and inherit my father's business.

Inwardly, I laughed. I had one purpose in mind. I intended to board a south-bound train that very day. Moreover, I despised the pleading tone in Snaith's voice. He was a born drudge in spite of his darkly handsome body. The height of his ambition was to exchange his poverty for the profitable little fishing business I would inherit from my father. But he must have been apprehensive about my reaction to his suggestion because at that moment he took my hand across the table.

'I love you, Helen,' he said.

My dislike increased. I detested him. But I smiled back at him because I was still, to some extent, at his mercy.

'Just as you think, Tom,' I said.

Relief came quickly to his face. He could be comfortable now in his betrayal. He squeezed my hand and helped me to another cup of tea. I glanced out of the window. Down on the street a policeman was bending over the parked motorcycle, peering at the number-plate. Then he took a notebook from his pocket and appeared to be comparing numbers.

As calmly as possible, I said to Snaith: 'Tom, do you think you would let me have some of the money back? I don't like to have nothing, and I'd like to buy some clothes for our wedding.'

For a moment he looked suspicious but then his brow cleared and he said: 'Of course, darling.'

He took out the money importantly and counted out twenty pounds, which he passed across to me.

I watched the policeman look up and down the street. Doubtless he was waiting for our return. I watched him move back out of sight into a doorway. My mind was already made up. I was going to allow Snaith to be arrested. Meanwhile I would make good my own escape. I told Snaith that I was going to visit the toilet and blew a kiss to him as I crossed the floor. Once downstairs, I left the restaurant by the side door. In the sunlight again, it occurred to me that there are some men whose necks are *made* for the rope.

I breathed a sigh of relief as the train drew out of the station, jerkily, until the carriages were properly disposed in motion behind the engine. I had been very nervous on the platform. Snaith would probably have been arrested, and he might have been spiteful enough to give the police information about me. But soon, with vast stretches of rough countryside rolling off into the distance beyond the window, I fell into a sound sleep in the corner of the carriage.

I woke up to find a young man looking across at me. He was clad in city clothes and was perhaps the most elegant man I had seen in my life. I flushed under his amused gaze. He blinked his eyes in greeting but said nothing. There were two other occupants in the compartment, an old couple, perhaps a retired farmer and his wife. I felt at once that they disapproved of me.

A hundred times during the day I felt the young man's eyes upon me, seldom on my face, more often on my legs or on my skirt or at the string which gathered the top of my dress in rucks over the smooth rise of my breasts. His attention, the insinuation in his eyes, and the throbbing motion of the train combined to make my flesh, damp from the journey, tingle with excitement against the undersurface of my clothes. Towards evening, I got up and went out into the corridor.

I moved along towards the end of the carriage to the little hallway which gave on to the toilet and stood looking out of the window at the dusk which was spreading to the pale orange horizon. A few moments later, I turned to find him standing beside me.

'It's a tiring journey,' he said in a pleasant voice.

I nodded.

'Trains are always boring,' he said.

I agreed.

'Do you smoke?' He offered me a cigarette from a slim cigarette case.

I took one although I had never smoked before. He lit it for me and laughed when I began to cough immediately.

'I thought I'd like to try one,' I apologised through my coughing.

'Good for you!' he said. 'You must try everything.'

At that moment, the train, which had slowed down, lurched into speed again, and the young man, knocked off his balance, came against me heavily. In his effort to steady himself, one of his hands gripped my arm, while the other, clutching lower down, closed on the upper part of my skirt, rending the material. Thus, suddenly, before both our eyes the velvety skin of my thigh was visible, pale and thickly fleshed in the gloom of the corridor. His apology was cut short by the sight of my face, turned up towards him now, my lips wet, expectant, and slightly apart, my glance boldly sensual. I was holding him close against me by his lapel. Without a word, he glanced quickly along the corridor and ushered me gently into the toilet.

For some minutes we pressed against one another with our straining bodies, our lips stuck together and his right hand kneading at the exposed flesh of my thigh; then, moving his hands downwards, he raised them again somewhere behind my knees under the skirt, upwards over the firm bulge of my buttocks, until, with one hand on either side, he clamped me close where his sex was. With the whole weight of my body balanced on the palms of his hands, I thrust my tongue deeply into his mouth, at the same time raising my legs round his waist, and then, in this position, he carried me across to the toilet seat, where he sat down, disclosing his sex with a deft movement, and lowered my rigid torso until I felt my cleft split by the blunt power of his erection. Such was the intensity of my desire, so heavy was the abandoned suspension of my legs, that he penetrated at once to the very pit of me. In that position, my long fair hair hanging untidily over my tightly shut eyes, I rocked deliriously with all the force of my lower torso. What had begun to exist as a dull throb of hunger in the hotbed of my flanks now concentrated to an abscess of stabbing pleasure in the utter profundity of my diaphragm and burst, shooting a delicious corrosion through every fissure of my flesh. Simultaneously, my nerves registered the final ecstatic vibrations of the strong shaft which transfixed me. My trembling thighs were wet with the lather of our fleshly collision, and between the smooth young globes of my tilting buttocks my glistening short hairs, still interwoven with his, seeped with a liquid like the viscous fluid of flowers. Under the wringing-wet shift his skilful fingers were tracing delicate patterns on my back, and the satisfied heap of my belly rose and fell against him for want of breath.

A moment later, he gently tilted my chin upwards and looked into my face.

'What's your name?' His grey eyes were amused but gentle at the same time.

'Helen.'

'Do you often do this?'

'I did it for the first time yesterday, with a man I mean.'

He raised his eyebrows in surprise.

'Where do you come from?'

I shook my head without answering.

'Alright,' he said. 'It's none of my business. Where are you going?'

'To Sydney first.'

'I'm going there too,' he said.

I smiled at him, drew his head towards me, and kissed him sensually on the lips. But he drew away.

'Not like that,' he said. 'Stand up, Helen, and take off your skirt.'

As I was wearing a dress I had to uncover the upper part of my torso as well. As I did so, the packet with my money fell out.

'What's that?' he asked.

'It's nothing,' I said. 'It's mine.'

'I don't doubt it,' he said casually. 'Now, put it down beside your dress and come here.'

I did not hesitate to obey. I was not wearing knickers. The upper part of my body was clad in a short shift of snow-white linen. It came down only as far as my navel. The soft burnished underside of my belly was thus naked except for the two elastic thongs of my garterbelt, which ran downwards to the fleshy part of my thighs, framing the gleaming hairs of my sex and joining the glove-tight neatness of my dull dark stockings, which caused the flesh to bulge slightly where it issued from them. I went towards him slowly.

When I reached the edge of the toilet on which he was sitting, he halted me. He sat for a moment, gazing at the warm contours of my mound. Then he stood up.

'Stand up there, Helen,' he said.

Again I obeyed him. I realised with pleasure what he was about to do. Level now with my centre, the smooth inclined place of my thighs sweeping downwards to his lips, it was as though some kind of erosion were taking place in my tired limbs. I quivered like a reed. A sliding within me mounted to breaking point as I clutched close, until the electricity mounted again to my nipples and the seed flowed in my womb like sand shifting in the tide.

At the peak of my pleasure, I moaned softly, uttering needless demands, the whispered words escaping hoarsely from between my lips until that final fractured moment when the orgiastic tensions snapped with the elasticity of a wet lip somewhere in the most secret part of me.

And there was more, with the sound of the rails underneath and emptiness in the corridor, before I rose to kiss him for the last time, but the train was slowing down to enter a station.

As I slipped the dress back over my warm satisfied flesh, the true immensity of the adventure before me filled me with an ungovernable joy of living.

Chapter Three

We must have come far during the day. But I saw very little except movement of the sand dunes in the strong sunlight. It was almost white. And, occasionally, a few palm trees.

They placed me in a kind of tent on top of one of the camels. Evidently they fear I might be seen by someone in a passing caravan. But the cloth flapped about in the air and I could see the swaying train of camels ahead, and sometimes a man on foot in a white burnous, or two or three of them, black-faced, sometimes turbanned, and occasionally a man would glance up at me. Each time I tried to see in him my lover of the night before. But I could never be certain.

Strangely enough, I feel almost no desire to escape now. I am caught up in my own history, which moves on hidden springs which I cannot pretend to understand. I suspect that I have abandoned myself so utterly that, were a chance of escape to offer itself, I would ignore it. I *want* the future that is in store for me. The discomfort of the day's journey is more than compensated for by the acute sense of anticipation which seems to hang at my thighs at this moment. It is nearly dark outside the tent. Not much noise in the camp. I will continue my account, but I shall have to be careful, for I may be visited at any moment.

I suppose what occurred now was inevitable. The nameless young stranger of the train – we agreed that we wanted to know nothing more of one another than we knew already – deserted me after a few days in Sydney, during which time he initiated me into some of the most subtle of erotic pleasures. He left the lodging house, where we stayed together as man and wife, taking most of the money with him. He left me only ten pounds and an unsigned note which read:

> *Dear Helen,*
>
> *You are a most wonderful creature and will go far. Meanwhile, with little compunction, I have taken your money. A girl like you has no need of it anyway, not, I'm afraid, that your need, had it existed, would have made any difference to my own very real requirements.*
>
> *Adieu.*

The theft was a blow. Stranded in Sydney almost without money, I was forced to give up temporarily the idea of my flight from Australia. I found it difficult to blame the young man, although I would willingly have seen him hanged to have my money back.

My inexperience, together with my desire to be near ocean-going ships, took me down to the docks in whose precincts all the flotsam and jetsam of the big seaport gathered. There, in one of the dockside cinemas, I allowed myself to be picked up by a man whose hand glided under my skirt during the performance. He was a sailor, and he took me to a cheap hotel in the neighbourhood. In the squalor of his bed, I surrendered to him all the delights of my young female limbs. He took me brutally, his massive body sprawled on top of my sensitive flesh, mouthing obscenities at the moment at which his lust parted from him. Afterwards, he called me a whore and a low bitch, doubtless because his lack of education caused him to be conscience-stricken by the intensity of his own pleasure. It was an experience which I would not have missed but which, in its unimaginative haste, palled very quickly.

He had promised to get me a passage to Singapore on one of the ships. In Singapore, he insinuated, a healthy young girl like myself could find lucrative work. I would earn enough money to travel farther west in comfort. It was only after he had deserted me for two days and two nights, leaving me utterly penniless, that I realised he had no intention of returning.

I had some difficulty in leaving the lodging house because my sailor had left without paying the bill. The landlord, a heavy man of nearly sixty, threatened to send for the police. He relented, but only after I had allowed him to take his pleasure of me in the cellar where the beer barrels were kept. He took me there to be out of the way of his wife, and, as it was a stone floor, he threw a few potato sacks down to protect my naked thighs. Afterwards, he drew two glasses of beer, toasted my health, and gave me a few shillings for my pocket. As I left, he patted my shoulder in a paternal way and told me to look after myself.

Free again, with all my possessions in one small case, I wandered through the narrow streets near the docks. I was held by the loading cranes which rose above the rooftops and by the foghorns of the ships which would soon sail for foreign countries. I had no idea of what I should do. I was beginning to realise the danger of letting myself be taken too easily. I had not eaten for two days and was farther off than ever from that soft narcotic climate in which I felt my whole being would flourish. Thus I repelled the advances of the various sailors who tried to pick me up on the streets, and finally I entered a quiet café, sat far away from the door, and ordered something to eat.

I had been sitting there alone for over half an hour, wondering what I was going to do for a place to sleep, when a young man entered. He was obviously a halfcaste, but he was very expensively dressed in a white silk shirt and a well-cut blue suit. He sat down first at a table close to me, and then, when I did not seem to notice him, he came and sat down beside me.

'Are you alone?' he said.

I nodded.

He smiled at me. 'You look unhappy,' he said. 'Have you anywhere to go?' His eyes were on the small case beside me.

I shook my head.

'Tired?'

'Yes.'

'You can sleep at my place for the night,' he said. 'We can discuss the future tomorrow.'

Without waiting for a reply, he lifted my case, paid the bill, and walked outside to his parked car. I had never seen one like it before. It was a new Jaguar. I followed mechanically. I was tired and desperate, and he looked more interesting than any of the sailors who hung around the streets, one of whom I would eventually have had to accept as a lover merely to get a bed.

We drove through the streets without speaking. Once only, his hand, slipping from the gear lever, fell onto my knee, and his grip tightened momentarily, but whether his gesture was meant to be reassuring or indicative of what he would expect of me I had no idea. His hand returned to change gears and the car drew up alongside a smart apartment building.

We mounted in the elevator to the top floor. There we entered his luxurious penthouse apartment which overlooked the city. A smartly made-up blonde maid, whose too-fitting black dress accentuated the sensual curves of her breasts and thighs, opened the door for us. She looked me up and down before her employer, in a cold voice, ordered her to take my bag and prepare the guest bedroom. She did so, undulating her plump buttocks as she walked away.

'Come and have a drink,' my host said when she had disappeared. 'Then you can have a bath and get cleaned up.'

He ushered me across the thickly carpeted hall into a lounge with a very low, pale grey ceiling, softly lambent with concealed lighting. The carpet was thick and pure white and strewn with variously coloured rugs. The walls, grey like the ceiling, supported modern paintings of nudes in erotic positions. The stone bust of the upper torso of a young woman stood on a draped pedestal in one corner. The furniture consisted mainly of divans, strewn apparently haphazardly round the room and covered with broad-striped red and white silk.

My host, who introduced himself as Tony, pressed a button beside a long mirror on the wall, and a complete bar, glittering with an array of liqueur bottles, swung into view.

He noticed my fascination, smiled, and said: 'What will you have?'

When I hesitated, he said: 'You haven't been in Sydney very long, have you?'

I blushed and shook my head.

'Don't worry,' he said. 'You can tell me all about it afterwards. Meanwhile, I will give you something very special.'

A moment later, he returned to me, holding a small glass containing a violet-coloured liquid in his hand.

'Drink that,' he said, his eyes hooded for a moment as his glance fell to where my young breasts, nervous under the thin material of my dress, rose and fell with my breathing. 'Drink it slowly. It will do you the world of good. And sit down, my dear.'

As I drank it, he watched me with a quizzical expression on his face. It was a sallow, handsome face, and his body looked strong and slim.

'Do you know, Helen,' he said after a moment, 'I believe that in the end we all get what we want . . . that is to say, if we want all that is implied in having any one thing?'

I laughed for the first time.

'It's easy for you to talk!' I said.

'But why?' he said in a surprised tone. 'I want all this.' He took in the room with a gesture.

'But what if I happened to want it?'

'Well, you are here. The place is for the moment at your disposal. Perhaps you will find you don't want it.'

'But I do!'

'We shall see,' he said slowly. 'Meanwhile, have one more drink before you take your bath.'

He filled my glass from the same bottle as before. As I drank, he moved across the room and switched on the radiogram. I settled comfortably on the divan and listened to the slow music.

'See, the bath is already filled!'

It was such a bath as I had never seen before, sunk into the floor and made entirely of black marble.

'You will look like Venus in that bath,' he said with a smile. 'When you have bathed, you will find your bedroom through that door on the left. There are clothes in the wardrobe. Help yourself.' So saying, he left me, quietly closing the door behind him.

When he had gone, I threw off my clothes. My naked body, reflected in the long mirrors which covered the walls, threw itself back at me from all sides, full, lissome, and gleaming whitely in bold contours. It was the first time that I had had the opportunity to see myself from so many positions. I sat on the edge of the bath, my thighs startlingly pale against the black marble, and then, softly, on the downy skin of my swelling buttocks, I slid down into the warm scented water which closed over my curving loins with a sensation of utter intoxication. And then I was lying at full length in the big bath, my pale taut breasts breaking the surface, my nipples mauve and opaque, like fat little buoys around which the water, in ever-increasing circles, moved gently away.

I washed myself with the huge soft sponge that had been left for me. The soap was smooth and creamy on my glistening skin. When I stood up, the bubbles, like sea froth, mingled with the fair wisps of my short hairs under which my mound, like the bulge of a tunnel, thrust itself forward, bearing beneath it a furled red flag, the sullen lips of my sex. Below them, in a voluptuous rise, my broad thighs gleamed like gold pillars, subtly shadowed where the smooth lines of my heavy muscles twisted obliquely in their strong growth, while my dimpled knees, like sunken water-lilies, lurked just below the surface of the water, which the discarded heats of my body had caused to cloud, so that my feet were no longer visible on the black marble below them.

Dried on the soft turkish towels which had been provided for me, I walked naked into the bedroom.

The ceiling of this room was low like that of the lounge, only everything in the room was white – the damask curtains, the silk-lined walls, the soft carpet, the dressing table with its vast curved mirror. The only spots of colour were the various articles of female toilet on the dressing table, the black sheets on the bed, and the gold picture frame on the wall, which was filled with folds of soft crimson velvet at the centre of which there was a gold tube, the shape of a horn, which contained a splendid white and purple orchid.

The wardrobe was a fitted one, contained in the wall behind a mirror. At first, I paid no attention to it. I crossed to the dressing table, examined the various perfumes, creams, and varnishes, and slowly, watching the graceful movements of my nude torso in the crystal mirror, I began to make myself up. First I scented myself all over, the tender surfaces of my thighs and arms, my breasts and neck, and the soft yellowish furrow between the impeccable globes of my buttocks. Then I began to paint myself – my nails, toenails, and lips, a bright crimson; my eyelids and the soft shadows under my eyes, touched green with silver; the various hollows of my body accentuated by touching them with gradual spots of yellow-green and blue-green; and my long eyelashes a jet black. Then I brushed my long platinum-blonde hair until it shone and stood back to examine the entire effect.

At that moment, a breath of wind parted the curtains and I moved across the room to the window. I discovered that it was open and that it led to a small balcony which overlooked the city. I lit a cigarette and stood in my woman's nakedness on the exposed balcony. I paid no attention to the men who peered at me from the windows opposite and only returned to the room when I had finished my cigarette.

The wardrobe next. I found there long dresses of various materials. I chose one of heavy silver lamé, slipped into it, and examined myself in the mirror. The dress was cleverly cut, with almost no front to it. Beginning at the navel, at which there was a finely wrought silver button, it was cut away downwards in a long spearhead so that it left the lower belly, the sex, and the whole taper of the thighs and legs entirely exposed. The train of the dress reached the floor and acted as a superb background for the starkly exposed soft front surface of the body. It was a strapless dress which left arms and shoulders entirely naked and, at the same time, because of subtle reinforcements, held the breasts high in two dully glowing silver cups. At that moment I had a brainwave. I found some silver ribbon in one of the dressing table drawers and, removing the orchid from its horn, I tied it neatly in position, just over and obscuring the strong sensuality of my mound. Then I stepped into a pair of high-heeled evening slippers and made my way back to the lounge.

Tony was reclining on one of the divans with a glass of whisky on a small table beside him. He shot me an admiring glance as I entered but did not rise to greet me.

'You must be hot with all those clothes on,' he said with a smile. 'Help yourself to a drink.'

When I had done so and was lying on another divan near him, he asked me if I was hungry.

'Not in the way you mean,' I said slowly.

'In that case,' he said immediately, 'we might have the show before dinner.' He got up, turned down most of the lights, leaving only those which shed softly on the divan on which I was lying, and then he returned to his own and made himself comfortable.

'What's all that for?' I said in surprise. 'Don't you want to come over here?'

'Don't ask so many questions, Helen,' he said. 'I'll explain everything soon enough. Meanwhile, relax and smoke a cigarette.' He threw one over to me, and I lit it with the lighter on the small table beside me.

The minutes crept by. I was exasperated to find that he wasn't even looking at me. He was lying back smoking against the cushions on his own divan, and he appeared to be thinking of something.

About five minutes later I realised that his glance was directed on a door to the right of me. I rolled over and looked.

In the doorway, the maid who had ushered me in was standing. That itself would have been strange enough. But that was not all. She was completely nude.

This big girl had her hands on her naked hips and was looking across at me sardonically. Her magnificent torso rippled as she moved, incredibly slowly, across the carpet towards me. My first impulse was to escape, but her slow movement and her eyes fixed on mine seemed to hypnotise me. I found myself powerless to move. There was a constriction at my belly and I breathed heavily. The luscious germinal juices mounted through my trembling thighs and my breasts quivered under the silver lamé. She was standing over me, looking down. I stubbed my cigarette and shot a quick glance at Tony, who said nothing and watched with a lazy smile on his lips.

Suddenly, without warning, she whipped away the orchid from my sex and cast it on the carpet.

Then, still without speaking, her fingers slipped quickly to the fasteners of my dress, which soon fell aside, exposing the whole front of my torso to her gaze. The tightness at my throat would not permit me to cry out. Terrified, I lay helpless and abandoned beneath her.

At her next movement, I resisted with all my strength. But the strange mask bore downwards, with the power of muscle, until I felt myself pinioned under soft and subtle gestures of fertility. A cry became a groan, fighting at impending thickness, a giving away. In response to the strange and extravagant intrusion which worked gently at the mastic substance which rose in my prickling hairs, my fists, which had pounded blindly, became relaxed, tensions cracked, and opposition died in me. The whole sheath of my lower torso was involved in the urgent systole and diastole of desire. I abandoned myself to the strength of my assailant and to the curious gaze of the man whose presence, felt rather than seen, seemed to cause my body to attain an abandoned luxuriance such as I had never before experienced. The sap rose under my skin. My legs, once tightly closed in their reluctance to take part in this unfamiliar orgy, became hot and flaccid as they widened to contain the gleaming oval movement of the woman's buoyant hips, and the soft cleft of my deeper consciousness was peeled as though by turf, exposing my dewy shoots which were radiant in abrasion. My mouth slackened, and my hands, which had been idle since resistance died in me, sought to participate. Simultaneously, I felt myself brought to the knowledge of a new seat of pleasure as one of her slender darts pierced the loamy oasis which heretofore had been innocent of all sensation. Riven now at twin poles of delight, my glistening torso slithered under discs, flats, and surfaces, under flanges of containment and protrusion, all seeking the weld of female unison. My breasts, charged with ambiguous alluvial sensations, slipped to and fro under their counterparts, and, at my sudden daring gesture, a shuddering groan escaped her and her reanimated body leapt with a soft smack on the limited gyration allowed it by the strong clamp of my thighs.

A moment later, before the huge symphony of our limbs had attained its climax, and before I had time to realise her purpose, she had ballooned about, bringing heat and darkness to my face and joining me in sweet and cyclic suffocation. At last, in that perfect circle of moist female passion, our plumes were spent and our bodies met in a subsidence of lavish abandon. Spent, tremulous, and glad, we lay there for some minutes, inhaling deeply, in a welter of glistening limbs.

'A delicious spectacle,' Tony was saying. 'Helen, I want to congratulate you on your quick wit. You were magnificent! And now that you ... eh ... know one another, allow me to introduce you. Helen, this is Ursula.'

We rolled apart.

Ursula laughed in a low voice. 'You're okay Helen,' she said. She pressed the white wet fold of my thigh.

'That's enough for the moment, Ursula my pet,' Tony said with a smile. 'Enough, as some liar said, is as good as a feast.'

He got up and went over to the bar. 'Now we'll have a drink and get down to business.' He returned with two long whiskies and soda which he presented to us, and then, installed on a chair opposite the divan on which we were still reclining in a nude state, he lit a cigarette and allowed his eyes to fall to the carpet. Presently he looked away.

'That,' he said, 'was by way of initiation. I suppose that is the first time you have made love with a woman. It probably won't be the last. Anyway, that is what I want to talk to you about. Believe it or not, Helen, there are here in Sydney many rich women who will pay a great deal of money to have a young woman.'

Once again Ursula pressed my thigh. 'It's easy, Helen,' she said. 'And the more they want, the more they pay.'

'A business like any other, naturally,' Tony said casually.

I said nothing.

He looked at me meaningfully and continued: 'The only difficulty is to find those women. It is not easy. But they exist. Yes, they exist, young, old, fat, thin, with only one idea in their heads. That is where I come in. I find the women and arrange the fees, which come directly to me. Ursula and the other girls do the necessary, for which they receive whatever is given them by the woman, money, trinkets, sometimes costly gifts, and a fixed salary and a wardrobe from me.'

They were both looking at me now, waiting for me to say something.

'You are interested?'

'I suppose so,' I said hesitantly.

'But there are a number of conditions,' Tony went on in a precise voice. 'I had better acquaint you with them before you make up your mind.'

'Oh, they're reasonable enough,' Ursula said with a laugh.

'The first is that you cannot set up in business for yourself, the second is that you must never let the customer know you are working for me – you do it because you like it, you understand? The third is that you must accept whatever assignment I allot to you, there will be no question of your refusing. The fourth, that you must be available at all times.' He hesitated, looked at me fixedly for a moment. 'And there is one last condition: you can't quit – is that understood?'

I looked at Ursula. She smiled reassuringly. I nodded. There was no question of giving up the present luxury. The future would look after itself.

Perhaps Tony doubted me, for he said next: 'I'd better warn you that one or two of the girls in the past have tried to quit. They are sorry for it now, you understand? They are no longer good-looking. They couldn't make a living as a whore at the docks.'

One again Ursula pressed my thigh. 'It's alright, darling,' she said. 'As long as you play straight with Tony you've nothing to worry about.'

Finally, I agreed. In that way I became for a time a woman's woman, the adored and pampered mistress of rich women who expected me to dress, speak, and act as they did. I moved in the hothouse world of scented boudoirs and flirted with the husbands whom I cuckolded.

Chapter Four

Last night no one came. Once or twice I heard a movement outside the tent and I hurried to conceal my journal. But no one disturbed me, so I was able to write on into the early hours. At the first signs of dawn I was exasperated. I have travelled a long way, emptying myself of whatever would not serve my insistent desire. To be denied, to have one's existence denied – are there not at least twenty men with the caravan?—is the most subtle of all punishments.

It is still early tonight. After an almost sleepless night, another hot day on the desert, nothing but sand, the harsh cries of the camel men, some mutton stew, a few dates, glances whose meaning I was unable to comprehend – and then, the oasis where we are camped now. The men seemed restless. I have a feeling that we are going to arrive somewhere soon.

I was installed in a small luxury flat of my own. I had been working for Tony for about six months. First there was the wife of a prominent businessman, then a German countess who was living for a short while in Sydney, and then there was a lull. I had been idle for the best part of two weeks. My salary was still paid. My mind, free of the cloying demands of rich women, was once again focussed on the possibility of leaving Australia. I had lost my fear of Tony. What, after all, could he do? I could be hundreds of miles away on the ocean before he even missed me. I had plenty of money to buy a ticket.

It was a fine morning. I gave way to the impulse to go immediately to a shipping office and book my passage. I walked there with a feeling of immense freedom. I had enough money for my requirements for the next few months. I had not a care in the world.

The shipping clerk accepted my money and gave me tickets for a ship which left for Singapore in ten days time. But before I left the office he counselled me to have my passport in order before the sailing date. It was the first time I had heard that such things as passports were required. He gave me the address of the passport office.

There, I made the stupid blunder of admitting that I was only nineteen.

'In that case,' the official said, 'your application will have to be signed by your parent or guardian.'

'But . . . my parents are dead.'

'Your legal guardian then, Miss,' the official said politely.

I took the papers home. I didn't know what to do next. I could hardly ask Tony's advice, nor one of our mutual acquaintances. And I didn't know anyone else except the charwoman, whom I suspected Tony had planted on me as a spy.

Two days later, Tony called me on the telephone. He said he would pick me up in about half an hour. I was a little nervous when I opened the door to him.

He was very pleasant. He said he had nothing to do and felt like taking a drive in the country. He would be glad of my company. I slipped into a two-piece costume and accompanied him to his waiting car.

Soon we were right out in the open country. Tony did not talk much. He accepted the cigarettes I offered him mechanically and concentrated on his driving. The car sped on for about an hour and then nosed up a little side road, round the bend of which a small farmstead became visible.

'Where are we going?' I said to him.

'A friend of mine lives here,' he said. 'We might have lunch there.'

As we drove into the yard, a squat man with powerful shoulders came out of the house to meet us. He was dressed in dungarees and looked like an ex-convict. His broad close-clipped head was tilted to one side questioningly, and his face as he drew near was twisted in a grin of recognition. He was a man of about fifty, with a broken nose, massive hands, and small close-set grey eyes which, as they flitted across my face, seemed to look through me.

He leaned down to the open window on Tony's side.

'Trouble, Tony?'

'The same thing,' Tony said in reply, and at that moment it dawned on me that he knew of my plans.

As he turned to address me, I found myself saying, 'No . . . no, please!'

'No what, Helen?' Tony said drily.

I didn't answer.

'Get out of the car, Helen.'

'You're leaving me with him?'

'Do as you're told!'

I got out. Tony followed me.

'Put her in the barn for the moment,' he said to the man.

The man gripped me tightly by the upper arm and drove me before him to a wooden building on the left side of the house.

'Keep your trap shut or it will be worse for you,' he said as he thrust me roughly inside. And then the door closed and the key turned in the lock.

It was quite light inside the barn. Oblongs of dust-moted light jutted downwards from holes in the roof, falling palely on the scattered heaps of straw. I sat down on the straw and lit a cigarette. But the fear of what they might do to me made me feel sick at the pit of my stomach, and I stubbed it after the first few puffs. I sat for several minutes thinking wildly of escape.

Tony stood over the brazier, watching the crossbar cattle brand become red-hot. Occasionally he glanced over at me where I cringed in fear on a heap of straw.

Duke, the squat ex-convict, stood over my naked trembling body, ready to prohibit my escape. The sharp texture of the straw prickled at the tender skin of my flanks, and my whole torso, glistening with a frantic sweat of fear, gleamed in a rigid curve under his lustful eyes.

'Go ahead,' Tony said suddenly. 'Do what you like. It will be a few minutes before this iron is hot enough anyway.'

No sooner had he said it than Duke leaned over me, gripping my upper arms in his powerful hands and forcing my shoulders back on to the straw. Rippling under the sweat, all the moulded muscles of my soft underside were thus exposed to the man's eyes, which at once fixed themselves on the nervous clot of hair between the lip of my belly and the podgy bowl of my tightly closed thighs. He released his grip to unbutton his trousers, leaving red splotches where his fingers had pressed into my upper arms. Then he bared his lower front to me, a powerful flower, stuck close with wiry black hairs under which his white skin gleamed moistly, like a mushroom in moonlight. At the sight of his desire, my fear left me, my belly and thighs took on the consistency of spawn, the latter opening as my legs arrowed at the knees, anticipating the bandit shock that would scrape the bottom of me like a ship's keel. Duke seemed fascinated by my arched hips, by the opaque tightness of my round little belly sunk between my broad upper thighs. He sank on his big knees on the straw between the hot scissors of my legs and, guiding his member in with his fingers, he penetrated me, until his hard belly was at mine and his chest, under his sweatshirt, was riding on the firm ballbearings of my nipples. I ran my fingers gently through his hair and brought his mouth against my soft wet lips. He groaned. With all the wiles of my imagination I gave him pleasure, meeting his onslaught with caresses and encouragement where he had expected nothing but violence and resistance, and soon his movements were transformed into those of a doting lover, and his body, as it rose and fell passionately, did so almost tenderly, as though he were afraid of alienating me and depriving himself of my wonderful soft connivance. As his male seed rose in his rod, his torso was shot through with a slow subterranean tremor, and, softening my whole body towards him, I cradled him into a long and delicately protracted erotic ecstasy. His seed swallowed by the warm sluice of my loins, I continued to caress him until his heavy breathing subsided and he opened eyes that were no longer the eyes of an enemy. I kissed him softly on the lips. He accepted the kiss with dumb bewilderment.

'Very beautiful!' Tony said ironically from where he stood by the brazier. 'Now get up, Duke, and let's get on with the business.'

I felt the man on top of me freeze.

'Quick, we haven't got all day.'

Duke got up slowly. He stood back and adjusted his dress.

Tony smiled ironically over at me. 'And now, Helen,' he said, 'you're going to be taught a lesson.'

The brand, in the shape of a cross, gleamed at the end of the pole. He touched it against a wisp of straw, which flared instantly.

'Turn her over and hold her down, Duke.'

'Aw, leave her alone,' Duke said.

I flashed a pleading glance at him.

Tony, noticing it, said: 'So you've fallen for the bitch, have you, Duke? Well, isn't that romantic?' He turned to me. 'You're going to be branded, Helen,' he said. 'On your left buttock. If you turn over and lie still, it will be over in a moment. If you struggle, you're liable to get burned in other places. Will you hold her, Duke, or would you rather watch?'

Duke glowered at the floor and said nothing.

Tony approached me with the gleaming brand.

'Turn over, Helen,' he said dangerously.

I stared at him and then, when he was within a yard of me, I cried out: 'Stop him, Duke!'

The ex-convict moved with a rapidity which one would not have expected in so heavy a man. Tony, turning to protect himself from the sudden assault, raised the brand at Duke, who grasped it at the haft in one huge hand, at the same time bringing his short thick knee up with incredible force into the other's groin. Tony, his eyes full of amazement, let out a horrible scream and fell writhing to the floor. Duke measured his distance and kicked out with his sharp boot deliberately at the other's head. It landed with a blunt thud. Tony twitched for a moment and lay still.

I stood up, still naked, and moved over to Duke. I took the brand, which he was still clutching at the haft, and threw it on the straw. Then I walked silently into his arms and pressed him against my warm body.

'Thanks, Duke,' I said. 'Now let's get out of here.'

'We'll take the car,' Duke said.

'Just a moment,' I said, and stooped down and took Tony's wallet from his inside pocket. Then, slipping into my clothes, I followed Duke quickly through the door. He went into the house and came out a moment later with a bag.

We drove quickly out of the yard, and soon we were heading at speed along the main road. 'We're going to Melbourne,' he said. 'I've got friends there.' Looking back the way we had come, I noticed a pillar of smoke rising from the direction of the barn. I said nothing to Duke, whose eyes were glued on the road in front of him.

When a man is involved in the warm chrysalis of a woman, the confederacy of motion, the mutual seed pleasures, can take place on various axes. We had writhed on soft gimbals in a hot seizing flux and reflux, quavering, vacillating, gyrating, hairs against hairs, mingling, sliding on soft graphite, passing and repassing, hips, shoulders, mouths, hollows, a navel to a mouth, a thigh to an arm, a breast between buttocks, the bellies slithering, until, after an hour of drunken love, we had reeled into a final position, each lusting for his spasm, such that I, looking down between the two smooth marble hillocks of my breasts at the hot shuddering tub of my chevron-tipped belly, saw, in my squatting position, my own greedy containment of the male thing, hard and perpendicular, from which I derived my pleasure. I was rotating slowly on the soft orbs of my buttocks while the man, very white under his crinkly black hairs, was lying in a prone position stark naked below me, his hands at my hips, abetting, urging my fluctuation. The big iron bed, the lair of our erotic crucifixion, creaked beneath us as his spike, gleaming with the silvery wetness of my passion, and my more soft insistent sheath met and remet, withdrew partially, and joined in the next and deeper thrust. Soon his hands fell away from my hips and his clenched fists prised themselves under his own buttocks to raise his phallic spine close at my furrow. This last hard movement, interpreted by my body as the symptom of the imminent emission from his, caused every valve of my carnality to be flooded with the juices of erotic sensation, and rising again for the last time on my dripping thighs, I brought the whole weight of my smouldering torso down upon the blunt thick spurting thing which clove me into delirium. At that moment he toppled me under him, and the hairs of his chest were like live terminals against the amorphous sludge of my breasts, while my greedy little belly shuddered against him in an effort to drain him dry. The tremors in my wrists, flanks, and calves continued for some time under the sweet suffocation that I continued to experience beneath his spent weight.

Later, I eased him onto the bed beside me.

'Well?'

'What?'

'You promised me good news, Duke.'

He grinned, moving one of his hands between the dripping softness of my thighs.

'Tonight, Helen,' he said.

I pulled him close to me, so that the tips of my breasts touched his chest and our thighs met.

'You mean it?'

'I'm smuggling you aboard tonight,' he said. 'The ship sails in the morning.'

'Where for?'

'Singapore,' he said.

I put my tongue between his broad lips.

'Take me, Duke,' I whispered.

His finger was already at work in the mounting juice between my legs.

Chapter Five

We are camped tonight near a town. Before I was finally led to the tent which, nightly, is prepared for me, I had time to gaze at the white walls, at the minarets, at the straggling dwellings of the poor which ride up the side of a hill.

Last night, for the second time, I was not called upon. The uncertainty of my existence is exasperating. I affirm that existence, nakedly and purely, through my sex. Or rather, it is affirmed for me by the desire of another to possess my body. Sentiments are death. I have shed them all. I want no part of them, want them to be no part of me. Apart from the mind which, for the last time, is taking the trouble to record the events which have led up to my new and purer existence, the mind which I shall allow to die as soon as the record is complete, I am only my sex, only thighs, belly, and breasts, ready to experience and to give experience, ready to feed, but more vitally than any of those subaqueous plants which, in the pale beauty which draws, destroy that which is attracted. My tentacles too are fatal, but only to what is not relevant, to what not carnal, that is to say, to all that is civilised. Mine is the true culture, all that is deep, all that is not surfaces; the pullulating sting of thighs, luxuriance, omnific – the only, and the dark fertility. How I long for the day, the hour when this journal will be finished, when, communication made, I can sink finally and be absorbed by the archaic part of myself, coming to be, surely, with the rising of sweet juices, as a sheen-haired torso only, in the maw of whose thick flesh lurks a terrible dagger of delight.

How boring the world is! Like a nun, I seek a place of retirement, wanting to meet others only on the altar of my wonderful religion, only in those dark rites in which the incense of my pleasure will be burnt. My genuflexions will be towards flesh and my litany will be those lust-inspired whispers that have no meaning other than to increase the teeming pleasure of my body's heat.

But what is exasperating is my inability to command a meeting. I cannot seduce if I am not near. No one comes. But, though I am temporarily unsatisfied, I am not afraid, for I suspect — the idea grows on me — that I already know my ultimate destiny. We shall see.

In the hold, on a mattress between two giant crates, I was very close to the throb of the ship's engines. Once a day Duke, who had signed on as one of the crew, visited me with food. He sat and watched me while I ate, and then, after I smoked a cigarette, or even while I was smoking it, he would caress me below my skirt until, fully aroused, I lay back and allowed him to take me on the mattress.

This went on for over a week. By that time we were far out to sea, ploughing our way towards Singapore. Then, one day, we were discovered.

The Second Officer, catching sight of Duke, his pockets stuffed with food, became suspicious. He followed Duke down to the hold.

There, just after I had begun to eat, he came upon us.

'You are a stowaway?' he said to me. It was almost a question, although, on a cargo ship, I don't see how there could have been any doubt about it.

Duke stood up. For a moment I thought he was going to attack the officer, but he evidently changed his mind.

'Duke, report at once to the bosun! Tell him to put you in irons! You, madam, will come with me.'

Duke, like a whipped dog, slunk away. I was never to see him again. When he had gone, the officer helped me up from the mattress and walked me in front of him towards the ladder.

'Will I be sent back to Australia?' I said nervously.

'We certainly won't put back for you,' he said sharply. 'Further than that, I'm not in a position to say what will happen to you. Now get going. You are going before the Captain.'

As we walked across the deck towards the stern, the eyes of the seamen who worked there followed me. One of them whistled. The officer ignored him. I followed behind him, finding it difficult to walk on the tilting deck on my high heels.

We climbed down through a companionway to the Captain's cabin.

'Wait here,' the officer said. He knocked and entered.

A moment later he came out and told me to enter.

As I did so, he closed the door behind me, and I heard him climb back up through the companionway.

I was in a fairly large-sized cabin, furnished with dark wood, hair sofas, and brass fittings. The Captain, a heavy, red-haired man with bulbous blue eyes in which there were red specks, looked me up and down from where he sat behind his desk. A map was spread out in front of him and hung down almost to the floor on one side. He was not wearing his cap, and his carrot-red hair stuck up in an angry shock on his head.

After a moment's silence he said: 'Are you Duke's wife?'

I shook my head.

'You're his whore, then?'

I flushed.

'Answer me, woman, what the hell are you doing on my ship?'

'I want to go to Singapore, sir.'

'Oho!' he said with a sneer. 'So you want to go to Singapore, do you?'

I nodded.

'This ... is ... not ... a ... passenger ... ship!' he thundered.

I said nothing.

'You couldn't pay for your passage?'

'Oh yes, but I haven't got a passport.'

'You haven't got a passport. And do you think they would let you ashore at Singapore without a passport?'

I didn't know what to say.

'How much money have you got? Put it on the desk!'

I took the money out of my bag and placed it in front of him. He gazed at it in amazement and then counted it. There was more than five hundred pounds.

'Quite a little fortune you have here,' he said more quietly. 'Where did you steal it?'

'I didn't steal it.'

'We shall see. Meanwhile, I shall take care of it. What is Duke to you?'

'Just a friend.'

'You're lying. A man doesn't smuggle a woman on board ship for nothing. You're his whore, aren't you?'

'We've made love, if that's what you mean.'

'What else d'you think I meant! You whore for him. You're his tart. It's plain English.' His plain English was uttered with an Irish intonation. 'What's your name?'

'Helen.'

'This is not a tea party, you damn whore! I asked you your name! Smith, Jones, Jackson, Green or Fauntleroy?'

'Smith,' I said quietly.

'Where are you from?' He had begun to take down the details in a notebook.

'Melbourne.'

'Age?'

'Nineteen.'

The questions followed one after another until finally he laid down his pen, blotted the entry, and closed the book. Then he stood up.

'You'll work while you're on board my ship,' he said. 'Get this cabin cleaned up. I'll attend to you later.' He walked towards the door.

'Will you let me go at Singapore?' I said.

'You'll be put ashore where you came on board,' he said shortly. 'The police will want to ask a few questions no doubt.'

It was late at night when he returned. He had been drinking heavily. I was sitting reading on one of the horsehair sofas. He swayed drunkenly into the cabin, looked almost surprised when he saw me, and then he leered.

'You stand up when I come in, whore!' he bawled.

I stood up.

'If you were my daughter, I'd flay you alive!' he said. He staggered over to a small cabinet and helped himself to some whisky. When he had gulped it down, he turned to face me again. The anger seemed to have gone out of his expression. His eyes dropped to my legs and moved up again over my haunches to my breasts.

'You're not a bad shape,' he said with an ingratiating smile. 'Sit down, girl. You'll take a drink?'

'I wouldn't mind.'

'That's the spirit! You'll find the old man's not so bad if you're accommodating.' He winked at me, staggered once again over to the cabinet, and carried a full glass of whisky back to me.

I accepted it with a pleasant smile and he sat down beside me. Putting his arm round me, he said: 'Drink up, girl, it's good for you.'

'I'm hungry,' I said. 'I haven't had anything to eat today.'

'Nothing to eat?' He frowned. 'Hold on then and I'll get you something.' He left the cabin.

Five minutes later he returned with a cold chicken and some bread. He sat me down at his desk and watched me eat. I was reminded at once of Duke who, daily, had done the same thing. There was no question in my mind that this sea captain intended to have me afterwards. That itself did not worry me. But I intended to leave the ship at Singapore. To go back to Australia was, among other things, dangerous, for I had every reason to believe that, if he wasn't dead from the kick on the head, Tony had perished when the barn caught fire. For all I knew, there might already have been a warrant out for my arrest. This would be almost certain if Tony had spoken to Ursula before he called for me.

'Will you let me ashore at Singapore?'

He did not reply.

'You can keep all the money,' I said softly.

'We'll talk about that some other time,' he said slyly. 'There's many days at sea between us and Singapore.'

I lowered my eyes demurely.

He chuckled. 'I'll think it over,' he said, drawing me onto his knee. 'For now, I've got other things on my mind.'

He put his hard calloused hand on the smooth curve of my knee, and his fingers under my thin dress worked at the rising flesh of my thigh. Suddenly, an idea struck him.

'See here,' he said, 'I've got a present for you.'

He got up from under me, crossed the cabin, and rummaged

around in a chest of drawers. A moment later, he turned and threw me a pair of sheer black silk stockings and a tiny frilly garterbelt.

'Put them on, girl,' he said. 'I'd like to see you in them.'

He sat down in an easy chair which commanded a full view of the cabin.

I undressed slowly before his excited gaze, slipping my thin dress up over my smooth thighs, off the superb thrust of my hips, and finally along the swan's neck posture of my arms. Soon I was completely in the nude, my full pointed breasts pouting freely in their firm silhouette. Then, slowly, I drew on the black gauze-like fabric of the stockings through which my creamy skin glinted with pale sensuality. Then, fixing the provocative garterbelt on the sullen weight of my hips, I attached the fittings to the tops of the stocking, bending my gleaming torso backwards and forwards to facilitate the operation. I stepped into my high-heeled shoes, took a deep breath to tauten the curve of my bosom, tongued my lips wet, and, with one hand on my hip, shot him a suggestive glance. He was breathing deeply in the tublike armchair, his prominent blue eyes transfixed by the delicate calix of my navel.

'Move!' he said hoarsely. 'Move slowly . . .'

The small smooth disc of my belly rose and fell with the graceful movements of my long satin legs and my full creamy haunches trembled with each step. Suddenly my limbs were invaded by the desire to turn myself into sex's instrument, and, rotating my hips in a motion of heavy sensuality, I glimpsed my powerful sex, at the centre of my white body, circling like a bee uncertain where to alight. I was imaginatively held by my own motion. The blonde fur of my mound did indeed become a bee which hovered around a conch shell which I lifted from the desk. Legs apart, a hissing sound escaping from my lips, my mound forming an arrowpoint to the long sleekness of my quivering thighs, I cupped the delicate form of the conch shell in my hands a few inches below my circling sex, hesitating with the whole dull tremor of my torso to alight on the shelltip. In this way, making mute love noises to the delicate urn-like thing I sought but refused to feed upon, I circled the cabin, sometimes with the shell at arms' length, sometimes nested between my firm-nippled breasts, occasionally grazing the secret fur between my legs, until, near the cabin door, I turned off most of the lights, so that the shadow of my convoluted torso fell softly about the cabin walls. Then, on my knees, the white wall of my belly thrust forward, my head toppling backwards, I brought the point of the cone to my face, hovered with it, and then took it between the lips of my mouth, greedily, like a child at mother's nipple. So complete was the metamorphosis of the conch shell that, still sucking the point violently, my whole body became weak with pleasure and I toppled sideways onto the cabin floor, where the garland of my excited flesh quivered on the darkly polished boards. Through the crescent rotundities of my female parts I felt my juices rise like a tide in answer to the shell's hypnotic influence. My fair blonde hair splashed about the dark wood, half-shrouding my strange sexual devotion. I rolled over on my back, the shell held like a goblet in slender white arms which seemed to be playing an instrument, slobbering on the brittle point in untempered passion. At the same time I opened wide my heavy female thighs so that the lips of my vagina parted, showing a pale wet ruby seam of complexity.

I heard a grunt from where the red-haired captain was sitting, and, rising on my elbow, I saw through my blonde hair, which fell in a smooth golden cascade, half-obscuring my vision, that his sex was out on his lap, strangely white against the ruddy forest of his short hairs. Slowly, I rose to my feet, still holding the conch shell, all the muscles of my slim body lustrous in the pale light, and brought my hands to my hips as my golden hair once again splashed about my delicately formed shoulderblades.

No sooner was I on my feet than I realised with vexation that the man was impotent. He was gazing down with a drunken look of awe at his own soft white imbecility lying on the nest of red hairs. I realised at once that the reason for this man's habitual anger was his knowledge that in spite of his desire he was no longer a male.

My vexation turned to anger. My whole body was crying out to be taken in a brutal sexual embrace. I threw myself between his legs in an attempt to rouse him, but he sat rigidly in his chair, staring glassily at his impotence. Then, with a sudden muffled curse, he grasped me by the hair of my head and twisted my lithe body backwards across his knees, so that my head fell backwards over one arm of the chair and my trembling thighs with their furry little diadem were exposed to his avid gaze. At the same time, he grasped the conch shell and thrust it brutally between the delicately lush cleft of my sex. I cried out in pain at the shock. The rigid conicular form was altogether too large for the smooth lovesleeve, but he held my sweating body in a firm arc and, with a relentless piston-motion of his forearm, he beat me into a low whimpering pleasure. My belly and flanks danced convulsively on his knees, and a warm protesting blood appeared in trickles between my love-lips and the hard indented conch shell, which was sunk almost to its maximum diameter in my vital centre. I groaned with pain as he eased the pressure in removing the thing which had split me, and then, his huge hands grasping me at the hips, my blonde hair forming a pool on the dark wood between his feet, he raised me to doting love, soothing the bleeding lips and causing the tearing commotion at my loins to subside in a soft corrosion.

He stood up, his mouth buried between the fleshy pillars of

my thighs, my body in its upside down position flat against his brass-buttoned jacket, and walked with me through a doorway into the small cabin where he slept. Almost gently, he laid me between the sheets, slipped out of his own clothes, and climbed naked and big as a barrel into the bunk beside me. He wasted no time. He inverted me quickly so that my dripping cleft was once again at his lips, his head resting on one of my voluptuous thighs, and with a gentle but firm thrust of one hand at the back of my smooth head he forced my face against the fleshy orchid that lay between his thighs. I was beyond resistance. Gradually, under the insistent caress strands of sensation spread like wildfire through my limbs, while my captor's member, perhaps because of the sadistic pleasure which he had lately experienced, perhaps because of the proximity of my now doting mouth, rose like a mast between his powerful thighs until its calibre, contained in the crocus of my hands, was such that I could resist it no longer. With a sinuous movement of my young torso, I reversed my position and my sex sought his. With a strangled cry of triumph he mounted me, thrusting his rampant member between the ermine-trimmed lips of my cleft, riding on my pneumatic breasts with his broad wire-haired chest and mouthing doting obscenities in the shadow of my abandoned neck.

I had never before experienced such overpowering strength in a male, and soon every tremulous petal of me opened as though under the rays of a ripening sun to suck in the sweet fluid that in the height of his terrible passion gushed forth with the thin pressure of steam. I thought that night that he would never allow me to sleep. Five times he mounted me, and five times my white body spread under him like soft wax, eager to expose the softest and the most secret parts of itself to the fibrous front which nuzzled it. At last, his arm coiled between my slippery buttocks, his mouth at my breast, and his broad hand at the small of my back, he fell into a deep sleep of contentment.

I lay for a while in the darkness, uneasy under the oppressive weight of his limbs, wondering whether or not I would be able to persuade him to allow me to land at Singapore, and then, weak from the night's love, I too fell asleep.

I was alone when I awoke. He had evidently gone on duty. I stretched and yawned and slid from the bunk onto the floor. I was amused to find that I was still wearing both the garter belt and the black silk stockings. The garter belt was torn, and it hung like a pretty kerchief on the gleaming flesh of my belly. The stockings were badly laddered, like those of a chorus girl in a cheap vaudeville. There were traces of blood on my thighs, but I experienced no pain in moving. I laughed at myself, dabbed my thighs with a sponge, and walked naked into the main cabin.

At that moment there was a discreet knock on the door and a seaman, bearing breakfast on a tray, entered. He had reached the centre of the cabin before he noticed me. At the sight of me, he stopped dead, his jaw dropping in surprise.

I sized him up quickly. He couldn't have been more than nineteen, and he had probably never been alone with a naked woman. If I could make a friend of him, he might prove useful – might, even if my lover of the previous night decided against it, smuggle me ashore.

'Bring it in next door,' I said crisply, and walked, with the slow swing of my graceful buttocks towards him, back into the cabin from which I had just come.

I sat down on the bunk with my shapely legs crossed.

A moment later, pale and hesitant, he followed me in.

'Where is the Captain?' I asked softly.

'In the chartroom, mum.' He held the tray in front of him, his eyes almost popping from their sockets.

'How long will he be there?'

'Said for me to tell you he'd be to see you in an hour or so, mum.'

I laughed softly. 'Put the tray down,' I said. 'And come here.'

After a moment's hesitation he did so, but he stood about a yard away.

'Closer,' I said.

He edged forward a few inches.

'Don't be afraid,' I said. 'What's your name?'

'Tom,' he said.

'Mine's Helen. Come closer and put your hand on my thigh.'

Wide-eyed, his hand quivering, he did so.

'Stroke it for me,' I whispered.

His hand, which had lain there like lead, stirred slightly, and soon his fingers became more sure of themselves and traced delicate patterns along the sloping inside surface of my thigh. But he remained afraid and caressed my creamy skin at arm's length.

The bunk was a high one. When I sat upright, my navel was on a level with his eyes. I opened my thighs like a book.

'Come close to me,' I said in a whisper.

He approached, fascinated. When he was close enough, I took his young boy's head close to my soft belly and pressed it there, running my slim fingers through his tousled hair.

'Put your arms round me and press me close,' I whispered sensually.

I felt his hands move slowly round my buttocks and soon, stifling sobs, he was burying his face in my belly. I went on caressing his head in a silence occasionally broken by a sob. An infinite tenderness existed in my veins.

'Come up onto the bunk with me,' I said in a tone of quiet command.

He did so without hesitation. I slipped my hand on his bare skin under his rough seaman's jersey and brought his lips against my left breast.

'Suck my breast,' I whispered.

His soft young lips closed round my nipple and the small exciting tug sent quivers of excitement down along the rise of my belly to the seat of my body's government. Patiently, I caressed his back, and then, drawing his legs sideways towards me, I ran my fingers lightly over the bulge in his trousers.

'Take them off,' I whispered.

Hastily he thrust his trousers away from him down to his calves. He was young and excited; his belly was almost innocent of hair.

The boy flung himself forward to bury himself deep within my belly before, in his first tense and vital excitement, his young seed out of all control coursed through his shuddering stem. No movement, no oscillation was necessary to set fire to his vital reservoir. He came in his first stroke as my voracious lovelips sucked him to the whirlpool of my female desire which, excited by this slimmest of lovers, caused the vice of my velvet thighs to contain him close till every youthful shudder had subsided.

I did not try to restrain him. He wished to be away from me. He was afraid. And I knew he would return. He would love me as long as I required his devotion.

'We'll make Singapore tomorrow morning,' the Captain said over dinner.

I looked at him closely, trying to read what was in his mind, but he evaded my glance. I had a definite impression that he would be unwilling to set me at liberty in Singapore. He had promised to do so by this time, but he avoided the subject as much as possible.

Captain O'Reilly had changed. He was no longer the bad-tempered bully who had confronted me that first time. He was now almost doglike in his devotion. He would have married me – he said a hundred times – if he had not already been married with children my own age. I believe he would have. That is to say, if I had agreed to such a preposterous match. O'Reilly was fifty-five and a poor man, king it is true when his ship was at sea, but just another anonymous little sea captain the moment his ship made port. As it was, he wanted me to be his mistress. The ship was far from home waters. Its home port was Liverpool in England. He could safely keep me aboard for at least eighteen months. He hinted at this so often that I began to suspect he had no intention of setting me free, and I congratulated myself on the secret love pact I had made with the callow youth who acted as his steward. Tom had promised to aid me to slip ashore at Singapore even if the Captain forbade it. I had cultivated him for the past week, giving myself to him each morning after the Captain had gone on deck, and he was now madly in love with me. I think he would have killed O'Reilly had I demanded it of him.

'You will let me leave the ship?'

'It may be difficult, Helen,' he said evasively. 'The Customs are sticky, you know. I'll have to look over the lie of the land once we get there.'

'I'm sure you'll manage,' I said gently.

'Oh, sure, sure!' he said hastily. 'Just give me a few days after we get there.'

I put my hand on his across the table.

'You know I'm in no hurry to leave you, John. It's just that I must feel free.'

'Of course,' he said. 'Don't worry.'

I was not worried. I had no intention of relying on him. As soon as he had gone ashore, I intended to make an attempt to land on my own. Or rather, with the help of Tom. O'Reilly wouldn't dare to lock me up. He would be afraid to make me suspicious. So, the night before we came to Singapore, I invited him to carry me to the bunk.

'Pretend this is our first night, John,' I said huskily.

O'Reilly was ashore. The dock was crowded with Chinese coolies and Englishmen in uniform. From somewhere came the nervous sputter of a pneumatic drill. The dockyard noises mingled with the hoarse Oriental shouts of the labourers, cranes turned, hawsers tightened, tug whistles blew. The docks were a kaleidoscope of colour, blue, red, green, yellow, and above this cauldron of commerce the sun struck down from an unbroken azure-blue sky.

Singapore!

Even the smells were different. As Tom dressed me in his clothes, I could hardly contain my impatience. Then he cut off the luscious blonde coils of my wonderful hair. I looked in the mirror. It was the face of a boy, albeit a pretty one.

'Wear the cap,' he said eagerly.

I placed it on my head. The fine goldspun appearance of my clipped hair was thus shrouded.

'And my papers. They'll get you past the policeman at the gate. Don't forget, Helen, somehow or other you must get them back to me. O'Reilly'll skin me alive if he finds out.'

'Don't worry, Tom. I'll send them back with someone and he'll leave word with you where you can meet me.'

'Promise?'

'I promise.' I kissed him on the lips.

'I'll die if you don't!'

I put the papers in the jacket pocket.

'I'm going now,' I said. 'Thanks for the money.' He had given me five pounds, which was all he had.

Embracing him for the last time, I slipped onto the deserted deck, walked quickly down the gangplank, and threaded my way between men and machinery towards the dockyard gate. Overhead, the giant arms of cranes swivelled with bales of merchandise. I hesitated to allow a trolley to pass. I intended to send back the papers, but I had no intention of seeing Tom again. He was far too sentimental – had he not buried his face in the cut locks of my hair and prayed me that he should be allowed to keep them?—even I could not have changed him.

The policeman glanced casually at my papers and allowed me to pass outside into the street. I had walked about twenty yards when I heard him call me back. Perhaps something in my walk had made him suspicious. I froze momentarily, and then, making up my mind in a flash, I dashed headlong for the nearest corner. I heard his shout and then the noise of his footsteps in pursuit. I turned the corner well ahead of him and found myself in an almost deserted side street. I cursed my luck. I had hoped for a main thoroughfare, for crowds into which I might disappear. I ran on. Fortunately, I was fleet-footed. My thighs flashed under the rough seaman's trousers. He was still about twenty yards behind when I turned the next corner. He was blowing a whistle now. I darted across the road towards a house which stood in its own grounds, almost running right into a rickshaw which moved swiftly across my path. I tore open the gate, slammed it behind me, and ran to hide in the bushes. I heard the footsteps of my pursuer turn the corner and come to a halt. He walked backwards and forwards in indecision. Cautiously, I crept through the bushes, trembling at every crackling twig, towards the low pagoda-like villa. In this way I circled the house. There was no one on the verandah which gave onto the lawn. I moved quickly across open space and slipped through the open French windows into a lounge furnished with all the splendours of the Orient. Silk damask, jades, ebonies and ivories, rich Chinese rugs, an atmosphere laden with the heavy-sweet smell of incense, which burned in a censer – I had not time to take it all in before I heard the sound of approaching voices speaking some Oriental tongue. I crossed the room in one bound and concealed myself behind some curtains of helio silk.

Chapter Six

We have been camped here for two days. A tall Arab came during the day with another man. He made me stand naked while the other man examined me, pinching my plump buttocks, feeling the posture of my hips, examining my teeth. Evidently I am to be sold.

The idea excites me. Not indifference, not horror, but positively and corruptively almost a feeling of lust. Here is a denial of personality which I have been at such pains to extinguish by my own efforts. Here is a positive and shattering assertion that I am coincident with the pleasure that is to be had between my thighs or at the nipples of my firm breasts. My wildest dreams then become for these men who handle me a matter of fact. Dualism is extinguished, mind obliterated by the refusal of these men to notice its existence. *I am annihilated.* There remains only this dusky front, the mould of this flank, the tilt of these breasts, the moist softness of this cleft below the strong jut of the mound. They have a life of their own, and in their alluvial silts I lust to submerge myself. And these strange men are my confederates. For the first time in my life, without hypocrisy, without prevarication, I am valued for what I am, woman, the roots of sex and pleasure. I am purged of all poisons, of civilisation.

From my hiding place behind the curtain I saw the two Chinese enter the room and sit cross-legged on cushions on the floor. A moment later a young Chinese girl entered bearing a tray with tea on it. She curtsied and placed it between the men. She was a doll-like, fragile creature dressed in heavily embroidered silk, a tunic, and black silk trousers. She wore boat-shaped little slippers on her naked yellow feet. Having placed the tray in position, she curtsied for a second time and glided silently from the room. The two men talked Chinese. Behind the curtain I leaned back well out of sight.

About a quarter of an hour later, one of the men clapped his hands. The same young Chinese girl entered and removed the tray. Then two fat little men, in dragon-patterned silk robes, came in carrying musical instruments. After bowing politely, they sat well back in one corner and began to play some kind of weird and apparently disordered melody.

One of the two spectators rose then and closed the French windows and over them the heavy damask curtains. In the semidarkness he crossed the room and struck one resounding blow on a brass gong. Then he rejoined the other man in a cross-legged position.

At that moment a tinkle of little bells came to me at the other side of the curtain. It sounded like the little jostling bells one sometimes finds on a pony harness. I widened the slit in the curtain to get a better view of what was passing in the room. A beam of green light from one side of the room picked out the smooth and heavily bedecked body of the young Balinese dancer whose sudden knee movements – for her knees were encrusted with small bells – had caused the tinkling sound which had caused me to look. Every movement of her green-hinged body was oblique, as though her graceful limbs were composed of mechanical jade. She wore a tall, intricately worked head-dress, which appeared to represent in a formalized way some personage in a nest of snakes. The snake-like impression was intensified by the cool angular thrusts of her arms and by the oiled rigidity of her long tapering hands. The cage of her pelvis seemed to be encrusted with jewels which in the strange light appeared to be embedded in the beautiful orbs of her buttocks and, in the centre of the pale green flesh of her soft twitching abdomen a ruby sparkled, a magic navel of fire which reflected the light in all its surfaces, sending needles of colour in all directions. Below the navel, the shadow of her mound was scarcely visible under the thin gold-metallic leaves which seemed to sprout amongst her slow-moving short hairs. Her breasts were entirely naked but tipped each with some jewel which sparkled faintly in the dance. Her neck supported a high collar of silver which lent rigidity to the poise of her head, the head of a statue, kohl-eyed and expressionless as that of an eastern goddess.

Under my startled eyes the strange dance progressed, continued rather, for it did not appear to have either a beginning or an end, being a series of gestures, exotic, sensual, and mechanical at the same time, and not a dance in our western sense. As the girl danced, I realised that her apparent height was deceptive. She was in fact extremely small, like a Chinese woman, and looked tall and stately merely because of the headdress, the exotic harness, and the lighting effects. She looked almost like a child or a doll, and her skin where it was visible had the sheen of pale green porcelain. Her hemispherical breasts were no bigger than apples, and bejewelled as they were, they glowed ambiguously with a fragile duck-egg blue. The faces of the men who sat cross-legged on the cushions were likewise expressionless. I was fascinated by the incense-laden formality of the spectacle.

Suddenly, as inconsequentially as it had begun, the music ceased. The girl stood rigid, without movement, her arms strangely crooked like the handles of an ornate vessel, her kohl-black eyes flickering and occult.

The fat little musicians got up and left the room.

One of the spectators bowed to the other, who returned his bow, and with his hands in the loose silk sleeves of his kimono, he followed the musicians out.

The man who remained said something in Chinese to the dancer. She bowed and sat down on the edge of a divan. Her face was devoid of expression. He crossed the room, did something with the light switches, and the beam changed the direction of its thrust so that the divan and the glimmering trappings of the dancer were flooded in a pool of green. Then he returned and sat down beside her. From my place of concealment I had a direct view of them.

They sat close on the divan, and, as he drew her towards him, the man's hand caressed the smooth naked slice of thigh which was now exposed to him. Then, with one hand behind her shoulders, he raised her head close to his own and kissed her on the lips. Their movements were slow and suggestive. He was breathing heavily. Suddenly he said something which I couldn't understand, at the same time relaxing his grip. The young girl slithered out of his grasp and began to remove her exotic trappings. First she removed the headdress, her slender arms pushing it upwards from her short blue-black hair. This had the effect of making her skilfully shaded eyes as large as saucers in which the strange liquids of fear and sensuality fought for control. Then, without a word, she stripped the bejewelled harness from her slim pale yellow body and cast it in a glittering heap on the floor, until she stood stark naked, as palely and supremely beautiful as a lily, her small silky mound like a soft paintbrush, wettened with ink.

For a moment he was content to admire her nudity and made no attempt to move towards her. She, meanwhile, stood with lowered glance, a delicate slave awaiting his pleasure. Then he reached forward to put his hands on her hips and drew her small body towards him. A slight reluctance caused a tremor to pass through her silken flesh before, abruptly, it swayed forward in complete subjection towards his lips. He kissed her navel, now devoid of its ruby, almost religiously, his hands cupped over her small tense buttocks, whose substance in the strange light quivered like pale green blancmange. Then his hands, caressing her sides and flanks, seemed to coax his own body off the divan. He was still wearing his kimono, which reached the floor around him like a tent. And so it turned out to be, for, hastelessly, his hands on her temples now, he forced her head and body downwards until she sat crosslegged at his feet, and, raising his kimono at the front, he brought it down over and shrouded her head and shoulders until she had disappeared entirely beneath its folds. They remained in this position for some time, and then gradually he raised her under his cloak so that her nude flesh must have been splashed against his front, while his hands – the kimono between them and her flesh – sought the smooth outline of her buttocks and her little yellow heels dangled just in sight below the hem of his kimono. In this position she rose and fell against him passionately, her toes flexed and sometimes finding the floor to prise herself forwards and upwards again against the unseen genitals of the man.

Soon they fell sideways onto the couch and the man's powerful lower limbs, naked and glistening in the green light, kicked amongst hers as his buttocks tightened to the orgasm.

They lay still.

A moment later he had divested himself of his kimono and was lying naked beside her. Already, I felt the familiar constriction at my throat, the subterranean tremor in the secrecy of my womb, and, had I not been afraid of his anger, I would have taken off my own clothes and offered myself to his embrace. As it was, I could scarcely restrain myself, for he had begun again to make love to her, only this time in an unfamiliar way. She was lying on her belly in front of him and his hands pulled her buttocks apart, exposing the soft downy crevice and the little amulet of illicit love, round and gathered as a rosebud. At that moment, I could not help comparing him to some horned and mythical creature, a demigod with a nymph, in a temple of initiation. He was kneeling behind her, between her legs. Cautiously, as one might thread a needle, he put his point to her, testing the elasticity of her nether love lips with small, almost doting hip pressures. Suddenly, he seemed to make up his mind, like a skilful surgeon who has decided how to make his incision, and, driving his knees into the softness of the divan, he penetrated her buttocks with the force of a battering ram. The girl cried out in pain but he held her. His forearm was a bar of iron at her straining shoulders. One hand held her by the tuft of hair at the scruff of her neck; the other was under her belly, pressing her rump upwards towards him, and his legs, like powerful creepers, grafted themselves to hers as he pinioned her helplessly to meet his thrust.

At first the girl lay unresisting like a crushed flower under the flat bow of his front, but gradually, as the exploring member moved more easily at her shy ventricle, her softened buttocks mushroomed slowly upwards towards their split to imprison what was within. In a subtle collusion of movement they knelt, the man behind and against the girl who drooped fraily forwards like a broken flower stem so that her glistening hair fell in a blue veil over her eyes. They came to a climax simultaneously, she, spiked deeply, sitting on his knee at the edge of the divan, her small oval hips tilted upwards and her lips, like soft red petals at his mouth, uttered a low moan of pleasure.

Almost immediately, he stood up, pressed a button, and the normal electric lights came into play.

He said something to the girl, who rose slowly to a standing position and raised her slender arms high above her head so that the flesh glimmered whitely under the thin wisp of blue-black hair at her armpits. Her buttocks were tight and her toes were tensed in the thick pile of the carpet. Her breasts and hips looked as though they were moulded of pale yellow porcelain, the former crowned by the buds of delicate violets. He nodded, crossed the floor to where the girl stood rigid in a quivering curve from her heels to her tilted breasts to her fingertips, and, without haste, ran the palm of his hand over the downy contour of her back and buttocks.

He seemed to wish to prolong his orgy indefinitely, to be unwilling to have the beautiful creature go out of his sight. He pinched and patted her with the fingers of a connoisseur. All the time she stood like a statue and I could hear him breathing heavily.

Suddenly, and quite viciously, he slapped her across the face with his open hand, so that she fell again across the divan. I think she must have fainted momentarily. When she came out of her faint she began to cry, low convulsive sobs which caused her little breasts to rise and fall tremulously. He raised her legs onto her stomach, opened her thighs like a bible and lowered his muscly front into the soft and shadowy cleft. The girl, stimulated by the contact, moaned and shuddered with pleasure, a pleasure which seemed all the more desperate and complete for the exaggerated sensitivity of her lacerated flesh. Shortly afterwards it was over. He threw her a pale blue kimono. She put it on, collected the pieces of her dancing costume, and crept from the room in a bowing posture.

The man, seemingly abstracted now, put on his own kimono, lit a long and tapering cigarette, and clapped his hands. The servant who appeared silently opened the curtains, flooding the room with daylight.

I was not able to leave my hiding place until evening. I was not afraid of my unknowing host's sexual passion. On the contrary, if my position in Singapore had not been so insecure I would willingly have given myself to him. But at that moment I was in need of a protector and not a lover, although I had no doubt that one man would insist on fulfilling both functions.

As soon as the room was deserted I had my first opportunity since leaving the ship to look at myself in the mirror. Straightway, I removed the cap and ruffled my blonde hair. It had a windswept appearance which, although I was unaware of it, was quite fashionable among Eastern women of that time. For myself, unconscious as yet of all fashions – in Australia clothes are worn to hide one's shame and not to render the female body more provocative – I was quite pleased with its appearance. But my clothes were impossible. Already I had conceived a plan. If I could find some suitable clothes I would not be afraid to be found 'in possession' of the room when the owner returned.

By a stroke of good fortune the matter was soon settled. I found an intricately worked kimono of brocaded yellow silk in a cabinet. Hastily, I divested myself of my seaman's attire, glanced at the luscious maturity of my creamy flesh, and slipped into the cool yellow silk. Then, rolling the clothes I had taken off into a bundle, I went through the French windows and threw it into the centre of a clump of bushes. The moment I had done so it occurred to me that I had forgotten about the young seaman's papers. They had been in one of the pockets. And now, since the undergrowth was so dense, they were irrevocably lost to me. But I had little time for the luxuries of conscience. Without delay I returned to the room and made myself comfortable on one of the divans.

About an hour later, a servant entered bearing a tray of refreshments. He had laid it down on a table before he became aware of my presence. His face remained impassive when he saw me. He hesitated for a moment and then, as though nothing was out of order, he left the room with small quick steps. I heard excited conversation at the other side of the door, high-pitched staccato Chinese voices. I got up from the divan and helped myself to a drink. I had decided that I might as well be hanged for a sheep as for a lamb, although I was tolerably certain that my host, obviously a man of culture, would be more imaginative than that in his treatment of me.

I moved over to a chair by the window to drink what I had poured myself, and I had no sooner installed myself there than the door opened and this prince of sensualists came graciously across the room towards me.

He stood a few yards off, bowed, and said in faultless English:

'You wished to see me, madam?'

'I need your help, sir,' I said.

'It will be my pleasure,' he replied at once. 'But first, my dear lady, hadn't you better explain to me how you come to be in my house, unknown to me, and wearing, if I am not mistaken, a garment which belongs to me?'

'I came in by the window,' I said. 'And as I had no clothes I put this on.'

'I see,' he said ironically, but never for a moment losing his affable tone. 'Like a goddess you arrived naked at my window, entered, and clothed yourself. Now all is explained.'

'I could hardly have presented myself to you without clothes,' I said with intended finality.

'Assuredly not,' he agreed most politely. 'A poor mortal such as I could not expect . . . ah, if it were only possible! But then, like my great master, Confucius, I am cursed by a restless and enquiring spirit. A fair goddess, in my house, in my robe . . .'

'If you wish to have it back,' I said with *hauteur*, and I began to take it off.

'Please, dear lady!' he said, raising a hand in protest. 'It is yours. You are more than welcome to everything that is in my house. Forgive my enquiring spirit! In some circumstances it is not the least of my virtues.'

I smiled at him.

'A moment,' he said, gesturing for me to sit down. He clapped his hands. A servant appeared and my host gave an order in Chinese.

'You will take tea, madam?'

I nodded. He beckoned to the servant who left the room. When he had gone my host sat down opposite me and said: 'And now perhaps you will be good enough to explain why you chose my house rather than another's and how you came to be in such an embarrassing position – I mean, it is highly unusual for an English lady to be out and about Singapore without clothes . . .'

'It was my husband,' I lied.

'You may depend upon my discretion, madam.'

'My husband is a Commander in the British Navy,' I said.

'So?'

'I told him I was going to leave him.'

'Ah!'

'He took away my clothes and locked me in my hotel room.'

'How ungallant of him!'

'I found an old raincoat.'

'That was fortunate.'

'I managed to get away by the fire escape.'

'You are a resourceful woman!'

'But an agent of my husband saw me and followed me. I ran and he chased me, but I managed to turn a corner and get out of sight. The road was deserted. I don't know what I was thinking about but I felt that if I could get rid of the raincoat . . . you understand?'

'So you took it off,' he said helpfully.

'I had forgotten I was naked underneath,' I went on desperately.

'A delicious oversight!' he smiled. 'And so?'

'Your gate was open. I slipped into your garden and hid among the bushes, but after a while I got cold so I came inside.'

'*Et voilà!*' he said. 'And now there is no longer a mystery.'

Although he acted as though he had believed my story, I had the unaccountable feeling that he was only pretending to do so, but I didn't really care. I felt sure he wouldn't send for the police.

'And now, madam, you do not wish to return to your husband?'

'Never!'

'And you wish me to help you? I count myself fortunate!'

'If only you would!'

'Rest assured I shall be your humble servant in this matter. You have only to command. And now' – for the servant had reappeared with a tray – 'let us take tea.'

My host informed me that he was a silk merchant, was Chinese, and that he had an everlasting respect for the British Navy. 'The British cruiser,' he said, 'it is the vicar of your great Empire. It answers the lies and iniquitous ambitions of your subject-savages with precision and relentless justice. A broadside . . . ha! Much more effective than words. Yes,' he concluded, 'I have the greatest respect.'

'I hope that doesn't mean for my husband!'

He made a gesture. 'There are ridiculous men everywhere,' he said. 'I am sure you had every provocation to leave your husband.'

I thanked him.

'No,' he said after a moment, 'I bring up the subject because I am expecting a young friend of mine shortly. He too is an English

Naval Officer, a Lieutenant in the Fleet Air Arm, perhaps you know him. His name is Hawkes.'

'I don't know him but I'd rather not meet him,' I said quickly.

He nodded understandingly.

'In that case,' he said, 'I shall put one of the upstairs rooms at your disposal. If you require anything you have only to ask.'

I thanked him again and asked him not to mention me to Lieutenant Hawkes.

'Of course not! My dear lady, you can trust me implicitly!'

He called a servant who conducted me to my new quarters.

My room, like the one I had left downstairs, was luxuriously furnished with carpets, silks, and brocades. There I found everything I required: toilet requisites, a private bathroom, and an endless array of Chinese clothes. I bathed carefully and made myself comfortable.

About nine in the evening a servant knocked and entered with dinner: caviare, chicken, and assorted crystalized fruits. I ate and relaxed with a cigarette and the local English paper which he brought along with the tray.

It was after eleven when my host appeared. He knocked quietly and entered.

'Mr Hawkes is gone,' he said immediately. 'I wondered whether you wished to tell me what it is you want me to do for you tonight or whether you wished to sleep now and talk about it tomorrow?'

I threw the paper aside. I had been reading of how the British Navy was collaborating with the local Customs in an attempt to put down opium smuggling which, it was said, had increased to alarming proportions.

'You were reading?' he said politely.

'Yes, I was reading about the opium smuggling,' I said.

'Ah yes,' he said after a moment's hesitation. 'It is an evil thing. Young Mr Hawkes is at present engaged in trying to track down the criminals.'

'Why is it so serious?' I said. 'Why shouldn't people smoke opium if they want to?'

'Ha!' exclaimed my host, 'it is interesting to hear a Westerner speak like that. The western vice is alcohol. You know it and therefore you are not afraid of it. We Chinese sometimes wonder what all the fuss is about.'

'It's people like your Mr Hawkes who make the world such a dreary place to live in.'

'Ah yes, poor Hawkes! I have often thought so. But he is such an honourable young man.'

'Why don't you sit down?' I said to him.

'If you are sure you don't wish to sleep . . .'

'I'm not at all tired,' I said.

'That is surprising after all you have been through today!'

'On the contrary, thanks to you, I feel so relieved!'

'It is a pleasure to help you. I begin to see, I think, that an English Naval Commander is not the type of husband who can hold a woman like you.'

I laughed. 'He's a fool!' I said.

'When it comes to women, is it not true that all men are fools?' my host said gallantly.

'You're not!' I said emphatically.

'Ah, my dear lady, that is very flattering, but on such a short acquaintance I don't see how you can possibly judge!'

I laughed.

'You see,' he continued, 'you don't know I am not a fool.'

'But I do,' I said, and then I heard myself saying, 'because, you see, I have a confession to make.'

'A confession?'

I nodded. It was too late to back out now.

'It is nothing that is not forgiven as soon as it is confessed,' he said charmingly. 'Of that I am quite sure.'

'Don't be so sure,' I said seriously.

'Well, you must tell me now certainly,' he said laughing.

'I watched you this afternoon.'

'This afternoon?' A shadow passed across his face.

'In the room downstairs with the girl, the dancer.'

'You were there even then?'

'Behind the curtains,' I confessed.

He hesitated. It was difficult to read the play of conflicting emotions on his face. He said at last:

'I did not realise of course that I was performing . . . I am alarmed . . . could not have known . . . I trust you were not too deeply shocked by my brutality . . . a way we have in the east, dear lady . . . another culture . . . a different view of such things. We are, perhaps, less squeamish, is that the word?'

'That,' I said, 'is how I am sure you are not a fool.'

'You approved!'

'I was jealous.'

'Jealous!'

'Why not?' I said. 'Do you think my husband makes love with so much imagination?'

'Would you want him to?'

'He would be incapable of it!'

'Our eastern manners please you?'

'What I've seen of them.'

'You are an amazing woman,' he said slowly. 'If I might be of service to you in that way . . .'

I looked at him. He was smiling inscrutably. But I felt his desire and my whole body reacted to it.

'I can think of nothing I'd like more,' I said as he took me into his arms.

Slowly, with an immense sense of fulfilment, I sank back on the cushions, drawing his small hard body on top of me. I felt the smooth skin of his face and his hot breath at my neck. Even through two thicknesses of silk I could feel the intense heat of his loins closely insistent next to my own. His soft lips burst suddenly open on mine and his tongue, unsheathing itself, began to explore the sensitive interior of my mouth. His skilful hands meanwhile sought my satin skin beneath the kimono and he stroked me softly, bringing the mysterious current to my loins by the slow caress of his fingertips. A dark pencil of lust seemed to move down from my brain to the quivering tips of my breasts and my whole singing body cried out to be taken. I moaned softly. 'Like this afternoon,' I said. Without waiting for him to reply, I pulled him from the divan, dropped to his feet as the dancer had, and naked, for I had thrown off my kimono, I insinuated myself under the hem of his garment. As I had suspected, he was quite naked beneath it, and as soon as the kimono swung over me like a tent, the air, hot from his male body, filled my nostrils, causing my head to move upwards as though magnetized between the powerful muscles of his thighs. He stood there, out of my sight, his strong legs astride and his hips tilting forwards and slightly upwards, and soon, in the utter darkness, I felt the rising violence of his passion. Above my trimming lips, his belly quivered against my forehead, and, a moment later, he moved backwards, guiding me with him, until he was sitting at the divan and I, still under the strange night of his kimono, my head locked between broad and fleshy walls, was his handmaiden, kneeling at his feet.

No sooner did I feel the rise against my doting lips than he brought me out into the light of the room again, stripped himself naked and threw himself on top of me on the divan. His hardness at once broke through the cleft of hair which shrouded the soft and singing weal. Mad with passion for him, I bucked my tremulous front against him to bring about the inundation. It followed almost immediately while he was prising my knees further apart with his hands. But he did not stop there. He got onto his knees and, grasping me by the calves, drew my thighs over his head until his face was buried in my hairy furrow and his tongue struck deep into my swimming sex. We remained in that position for some time, his mouth exploring my female intricacies and his hands, like starfish, cradling the mellow globes of my buttocks, pressing them toward him to aid the penetration. Then his mouth quitted its task and there existed a lecherous rudder between my excited buttocks searching for the little studlike amethyst between them. Meanwhile, his fingers caressed towards that new centre, and I felt the tips of them play delicately with the mastic ring through which, with a gust of anticipation, I realised his courage would soon pass. As his fingertips played there, I clenched and unclenched the muscles which caused it to dilate and contract in lust. Noticing my movement, he thrust his thumb into me, quite brutally. For a moment I lay still, feeling without moving the presence of the flesh in my flesh. A prickling prescience overtook me. Then, cautiously, by dilating and contracting again, I began to feel into the oscillation I was soon to experience. When he saw my reaction he removed his thumb and turned me over on my trembling belly. I closed my eyes into the cushions. Everything was silent. The desire for the new pain which would bring the terrible pleasure into my body made me feel weak, tensionless, dragged downwards from the roots, like a flag drooping in a windless atmosphere. Once again I felt his fingers examining the orifice, then, gently, he pulled my sweating buttocks apart and laid his smoothness on the puckered indentation. I held my breath. One of his hands passed under the warm curve of my belly, his middle finger finding my cleat. His other hand grasped me by the hair at the back of my neck and his forearm bore heavily down on my tense shoulder muscles. By moving my body slightly I realised that I was now pinioned helplessly before his lust. There was no way of escape. Indeed, I wanted to escape and give myself at the same time. Now I was able to understand the presence of the elements of fear and desire in the eyes of the Chinese concubine. I had no further time to think. Suddenly, with the force of a ramrod, the cylinder burst into me and buried itself up to the hilt in my quivering buttocks. I cried out in pain and made a desperate attempt to buck him off, but by that time his legs had closed in relentlessly like octopus' tentacles at my calves and his hand tightened its grip at the scruff of my neck and soon, in spite of my whimpering resistance, his rod sheathed and unsheathed itself inexorably like a radiant coal at my tender flesh. Gradually, I accepted the pain. It lost its tearing quality. And soon, without consciously attempting to offer compliance, I felt my buttocks rise and fall like bobbing corks against his moving front. It was no longer painful. This illicit part of me was now as voracious as my mouth had been. I wanted him to sink deeper to accomplish his primal movement in the darker recesses of my abdomen. When he finally did so, I was beside myself with desire. Every muscle, every tissue of my body was crying out for punishment.

I thrust my arms with hands clasped above my head where I lay, inviting him to hurt me. He did not hesitate, did not caress first as he did with the Chinese girl. My body was rigid, locked, as it were, by tendons which radiated to the extremities of my limbs from the anchor of my sex. My muscles were hard and flexed. All my female softnesses were a bank of flowers awaiting fertilisation. I cried out, not knowing whether it was for pain or joy, and, before I had time to protest or to resubmit myself, I felt myself turned over roughly and a sudden searing sensation struck my belly.

At that moment, he set himself at me firmly, his body a strong wall of muscle and heat, and his male organ struck again, driving deep to my roots. We reached our final orgasm within a split second of one another, and, as I felt the rigid arc of his body thrust downwards for the last time, all the pains and the exquisite pleasure of my ravishment made me utterly delirious. I cried out like a Turk, arched my body in a supple bend, and collapsed almost unconscious under the foreign weight. But soon his lips were at mine again, and my tears of pain were stifled against his neck and shoulders as his skilful fingers, playing at my battle scars, induced a tingling pleasure which passed through my prostrate frame in waves of contented shudders. I took one of his thighs between mine and squeezed it. My senses swam and I fainted.

'This, my dear Helen, is Mr Hawkes, whom I have already spoken to you about.'

Lieutenant Hawkes, a tall young man in his late twenties, was in civilian clothes. He shook hands in a formal way with a slight bow.

'I have told my guest in what high esteem I hold the British Navy,' said my host with a smile.

'Oh yes?' Hawkes said vaguely. I felt that in spite of his *obvious* coolness towards me, young Mr Hawkes was more interested in me than he would have admitted.

A week had passed since I first entered the house, and during that time I had lived in the midst of a luxury which was almost incredible. Every demand had been satisfied. The presence of Lieutenant Hawkes was the climax, and indeed heralded the end of my delightful stay. It was the opinion of the host that I would not be safe until I was out of Singapore, safe that is from the agents of my 'husband,' for I had never gone back on my original story. To this end, Lieutenant Hawkes, who had just been granted two weeks leave from his arduous duties with the Fleet Air Arm, had been prevailed upon by his rich friend to fly me in a private aeroplane beyond the reach of the man who was supposed to be looking for me. Or so anyway I thought at the time – but more of this later.

This evening we were to have dinner together so that the young man and myself could get to know one another and arrange the details of the flight. Beneath my outward calm I was slightly nervous. Hawkes, after all, would know most of the English officers in Singapore, and he might suspect that my story was a mere fabrication. At dinner, therefore, while playing with the long crystal stem of my wine glass, I took the risk of putting the question to him:

'You don't know my husband by any chance, Mr Hawkes?'

'Your husband?' He was smiling with an air of amused surprise.

'Commander X!' said my host sharply to his young friend, and I had the impression that his tone of voice intended to quell the young man's high spirits.

It certainly had that effect, because Hawkes blushed and stammered: 'I'm so sorry, madam, I was thinking about something else. I mean no, you see there are so many naval officers in Singapore one can hardly be acquainted with them all, and anyway I have never been let into the secret of who he is, I mean his name.'

'Of course,' said my host smoothly, 'unless he happened to be a personal friend of yours you would hardly be able to identify him without a name to go on. I don't suppose the unfortunate fellow would advertise it in the news bulletin at the base! A dog perhaps! But a beautiful young woman of whom, I fear, he is exceedingly jealous! No. He will want to keep this news to himself. An enquiry agent perhaps. Such men are used to discretion, that is what they are paid for. In the mess I am quite sure you will not be reported as missing, my dear. You have gone to visit your mother, no doubt, or a maiden aunt. A man does not advertise his shame!'

'How well you know John!' I laughed. 'No. He won't have said a word to anyone. Think of it, Mr Hawkes: he might be your own Commanding Officer!'

Hawkes' laugh was forced.

'Hardly that, my dear,' my host said in a propitiating tone. 'Mr Hawkes is a pilot. Your husband is a seaman, a deck officer.'

'Of course I was only joking,' I agreed. I decided I had said enough about my 'husband.' Although I didn't see now that it mattered since I was sure of my host's, my lover's goodwill, I had no wish to commit a *faux pas*. I was quite ignorant, more ignorant than a real Commander's wife would have been, of navy affairs.

At that moment, fortunately, my host changed the subject.

'And now, Hawkes, we must discuss the lady's journey. You have flown before, my dear?'

I shook my head.

'Well, a long journey in a small plane will certainly be an experience for you.'

'We set out at dawn as arranged?' Lieutenant Hawkes asked.

'Tomorrow morning?' I said with some surprise.

My host laid his hand on mine across the table.

'The sooner you go, the sooner you'll be safe, my dear.'

'Your papers are in order?' Lieutenant Hawkes asked me.

My host replied for me. 'Quite in order,' he said with finality.

'In that case,' Hawkes said, 'tomorrow morning's as good as any. I don't want to hang about Singapore for my leave.'

'Quite so,' the other replied. 'Mr Hawkes, my dear, is going to fly you as far as Calcutta, quite a distance, some 2,000 miles. You will of course break the journey, twice in fact, once at Bangkok and again at Rangoon. From Calcutta you can go where you want, by boat or train or in an ordinary passenger plane. Mr Hawkes will not have time to take you farther. It is fortunate,' he added meaningfully, 'that you were able to bring your passport with you when you left your husband. I shall give it to Mr Hawkes before you set out in the morning.'

The remainder of the meal passed very pleasantly. About ten o'clock, my host suggested that I should retire so as to be fresh for the morrow's journey. I did so gladly, hoping for once that my host would not visit me in my bedroom, because after a week's violent lovemaking my whole body ached with fatigue.

I fell asleep quickly and I was not disturbed.

The engine droned steadily. Below was the flat studded plain of a huge sea which stretched in all directions as far as and beyond the eye's power of vision. Hawkes was even less talkative than he had been the evening before. He sat at the controls in wooden silence, his face set grimly and his lean body relaxed.

I had been studying the map. We had left the land behind us in less than two hours, and its disposition as it disappeared in a purplish haze puzzled me. It seemed to me that if we flew across the sea at all en route for Bangkok we should leave land on, and not far on, the left. As it was, we were now out of sight of land altogether, and, what was even more strange, we had seemed to fly above a very broad channel, leaving land to both sides of us as the channel widened into sea. There had been a number of ships, like toys bobbing in the ocean, but now, for the best part of an hour, there was nothing but the ominous endlessness of deep green sea.

'Are you sure we're going the right way, Mr Hawkes?'

'Yes.' He didn't even turn to answer. He was looking straight ahead. I felt, somehow, that he was tense and nervous.

'What I can't understand,' I said, pushing the map in front of him, 'is how we left the land behind us. It doesn't seem right according to the map.'

'What do you mean?'

'Well, we should have left the land behind us to the left.'

'We did,' he said briefly.

'We didn't!' I said in alarm.

'Do you think I don't know how to navigate?'

I didn't know what to say.

'Perhaps you'd better take over,' he said sarcastically.

But I had begun to be afraid.

'There was land to left *and* to right of us,' I said.

'Look,' he said tonelessly, 'if you think you can fly this plane better than I you'd better take over.' With that he pushed the steering column forward and released his grip on the controls. The plane gave a sickening lurch forward and downwards, and in a fraction of a moment, as he kicked one foot forward, twisted into a spin. I screamed and closed my eyes. How long we went downwards I don't know. I remember only that the spinning motion stopped and gradually with a terrible relentless motion the nose of the plane came upwards almost, it seemed, out of the sea. And then we were flying low over the water at what appeared at that level to be an incredible speed.

'Had enough?' I heard him say.

'You damn fool!' I shouted angrily above the roar of the engine. 'What do you think you are doing?'

He didn't reply. He nosed the plane upwards and slowly we gained height until we were flying at approximately the same height as before.

'Who the hell are you, anyway?' he said suddenly.

'What do you mean?'

'Come off it,' he said drily. 'Do you think I like doing this?'

'What?'

'The game's up,' he said, still without looking at me. 'There's no use shamming anymore. Look,' and his voice was gentle suddenly, 'I'm sorry to have to do this, really. You're a brave woman. I respect you. But this is no time for tomfoolery.'

'I don't know what you mean,' I said.

He shook his head hopelessly. 'Look below you,' he said. 'Do you see any ships?'

'No.'

'So you haven't a chance, have you?'

I was terrified. He was looking at me now, not unkindly.

'What are you saying?' I said, almost in tears.

'Can I do anything for you? I can do it anonymously when I get back. Look, for God's sake take a hold of yourself. You knew damn well what a dangerous game you were playing. Alright, you've lost. The next one might have more luck, and then it will probably be my turn. And then, later on, his. They'll get him sooner or later.'

I broke into tears. 'Please Mr Hawkes! I don't understand! What are you going to do to me?'

His handsome face turned towards me again and his grey eyes were gentle. 'If it will make it easier for you,' he said tenderly, 'I'll shoot you first. But anyway, you'll be dead by the time you hit the water.'

'For God's sake tell me *why*!'

'You make it very difficult for me,' he said. 'You must have known your job was dangerous.'

'What job?'

'Oh, for God's sake cut it out!' he said. 'Do you think we believed your Commander's wife story for a minute? Really, I didn't think the authorities could be so naive. Your job was suicide.'

'You must listen to me!' I said desperately. 'You must believe me! I don't know what you're talking about!'

He looked at me incredulously.

'Are you trying to tell me you are not an agent of the British government?'

'Of course I'm not! Don't you see?'

His expression was perplexed. 'I almost believe you,' he said.

'You *must* believe me!'

For a long time he was silent.

'I believe you are telling the truth,' he said at last.

'Oh, of course I am!' I began to say, but he cut me short.

'Quickly,' he said, 'tell me who you are and what you were doing in Chen's house.'

As briefly as possible I told him the history of my adventures since leaving my home village in Australia, how I had run away from home, given myself to men, travelled thousands of miles to arrive finally, almost desperate, in Chen's garden. He did not press me for details about my sexual affairs but his lips loosened in a soft, nakedly sensual smile. And then he laughed. Turning to face me, he said:

'You must prove it to me, Helen.'

'How?'

'Have you ever made love in an aeroplane?' he said.

I shook my head.

He laughed softly. 'Take off your clothes, Helen,' he said.

'Sit astride my knees,' he said.

I was standing beside him, completely naked. My clothes lay in a small heap by the side of his seat. His right hand, reaching to the cabin floor, stirred amongst my still-warm silk scanties.

'How warm your clothes are!' he said, and his hand moved upwards from the discarded silks to the warmer, more living silken surface of my inner thigh. He pulled me gently towards him, raising his hand under the heavy substance of my thigh so that my leg swung over his knees and I had only to sit to bring my warm belly and the smooth-haired lip of my mound against his own parts, which he had bared with his free hand. With the other, he still controlled the flight of the plane, west-wards, across the vast waters of the Bay of Bengal. For, of course, I had not been wrong. We had travelled northwest from Singapore through the straits between Malaya and Sumatra, out above the open sea. With the hand which controlled our flight he pulled me closer to his lower belly, his hand pressing against the smooth globes of my buttocks. His other hand, meanwhile, brought his excited member against the entrance to the cave of all my feeling. When he was satisfied with our position, the hand which had pressed me towards him returned to the controls, easing gradually back on the steering column so that my wet and pulsing vagina, parted at its extremity by his thrusting manhood, contained him suddenly like a glove. Up, up, up, the weight of my own flesh causing me to be spiked more deeply against the sudden upward motion of the plane. As we climbed, my whole body lay on top of his and his free hand, calmly and with the skill of a fine pilot, brought my head and my lips against his. We lay there, making an acute angle with the horizontal, our eyes open in the bright blue daylight which swamped us through the windows of the cabin, while little scudding wisps of cloud fell away below us at either side. As yet, we had hardly moved. It was the movement of the aeroplane which caused the creeping accumulation at our loins. His feet worked skilfully at the rudder bars, tilting the plane and causing my torso to swivel voluptuously against his, our bellies grazing languorously and the shock of the meeting of our bodies absorbed by the resiliency at my breasts. Our bodies, together in illusory suspension in the wide ether, absorbed all space, the lure of stars, flesh chucked minutely against flesh in this strange carnal confluence. His strong warm lower belly in its tilted position was the fang of a vast upward propulsion, raking with its fleshy dagger at the warm and viscous bin of lust which I lowered around his desire. Out of the world he seemed to drive me, beyond laws of motion, with the white ether streaming downwards with no velocity. The shifts, the slips, the slides, the slithers, the glides, the rolls did not move so much as concentrate a stranded passion, a still aerial conjunction which increased as the belly surfaces, fused by some aerostatic law, shuddered and sang above our wet sexual confusion. I could happily have ridden there pricked by this man's passion until the world's end, but, alas! that was not to be, for at that moment, when the seeds shifted for the thousandth time in my craving womb, Hawkes' soft voice came to me:

'Have you ever been beyond choice, Helen?'

The earnest seriousness of his voice brought me back to the world. My eyes read 17,000 feet on the altimeter, saw again the trailing wisps of cloud and came finally to rest on the grey eyes which looked upwards into mine with a questioning look.

I ran my fingers through the soft brown hair which framed the handsome face, the face of a flier, a dangerous man, a criminal, perhaps a traitor, but the face of a man with whom in the short space of an hour I had fallen violently and irrevocably in love. Here at last, I felt, was a man to whom I would be willing to surrender not only my body but my freedom. For the first time in my life, I felt then, I had met a man who was worthy of me. For an hour he had careened about the sky with me, controlling every tremor of our love with his wrist. I didn't answer him. I pulled his lips upwards against mine and kissed him with all the doting passion at my command. It was I who spoke next.

'Who is Chen, darling?'

He laughed harshly.

'Chen is a kind of king, darling. He controls the drug traffic in southeast Asia.'

'And you?'

'One of his pawns,' he said with a quiet smile. 'I do as I'm told, double-cross the Navy, and am tolerated because I'm useful. You see, I'm one of the naval pilots who have been lent to the Customs House to track down the head of the drug ring.'

'And he told you to get rid of me?'

'Yes,' he said quietly.

'Are you glad you didn't?'

He dropped his eyes. 'You don't understand, Helen,' he said. 'That's what I was trying to say about being beyond choice.'

'What do you mean, darling?'

'I *have* got rid of you.'

'How?'

'I had no choice, Helen. When I made love to you I signed our death warrants. He would have killed me if I had taken you back, killed us both. I should have dropped you a while back. You see, my darling, there is not enough petrol to return to land. Another ten minutes and the tank will be empty.'

The grey eyes were looking into mine, calm and without fear. Even this sudden and shocking news of my impending death could not shatter the wonderful illusion of fulfilment. I lowered my lips onto his, brushing them merely with the wet full curves of my own, and then, my mouth whispering in his ear, doting, trembling, I uttered the words: 'Fuck me again, darling, now . . . before it's too late . . .'

I was still astride his naked thighs when the engine sputtered into silence. I burst into tears and tried to move away.

He said: 'Stay where you are, Helen, this is the best way to die. There's nothing we can do.'

Then began the long swift glide downwards through the scudding wisps of cirrus clouds, and the sea, like a vast inverted green-black saucer, moved upwards to meet us.

'Don't turn, darling,' he said quietly. 'I'm going to bring her down as smoothly as I can.'

The sea at the windows on either side raced past like a vast and glittering black ribbon. As the plane lurched to alight, I threw my arms around his neck and crushed his head with all the strength of my torso against my naked breasts. The aircraft shuddered, slewed, somersaulted, and then, in a fraction of a second . . . blackness.

INSERTION BY MAJOR PIERRE JAVET, ADJUTANT, GHARDAÏA.

I regret the necessity of having to interrupt the account of Mlle. Helen Smith at this point. Unfortunately, there appear to be a number of sheets missing from the manuscript.

The Arab denies all knowledge of these missing pages. He found the manuscript, he says, as it stands. All our attempts at 'persuasion' have been of no avail. Thus, at a critical point in the amaʒing document, we are left, to risk a figure of speech, 'in the air!' In the water, rather, for the small aircraft must have hit the water to have somersaulted in such a manner.

This is unfortunate in two ways. In the first place, the continuity of the woman's trek across the desert with the caravan is interrupted. When we take her up again, she seems to be installed in what I imagine is some kind of brothel, and we are thus deprived of pages in which the last stages of her journey might, through her descriptions, have taken on real geographical reference. That is to say, she might have described some well-known landmark whose presence in the manuscript would have led us to trace her whereabouts quickly and efficiently. As it is, progress in our investigations is, at least temporarily, blocked.

Secondly, the continuity of the document as it pertains to her crash into a shark-infested sea with the young naval officer, Hawkes, and her subsequent appearance in the middle of India, is broken. How she escaped from that plight, and whether or not Hawkes perished (this latter appears likely because of a later reference in the manuscript to the young pilot) we shall perhaps never know.

An interesting sequel, however. Information passed on to the British government about the character Chen has already led to his arrest and conviction on a charge of wide-scale opium smuggling in southeast Asia. Other facts have already been checked by the various governments concerned and every item of information (e.g. the burning alive in a barn not far from Sydney of a man called Tony Sulla, next to whose body was found a branding iron, and in whose flat was discovered correspondence which led to many subsequent arrests) has been corroborated.

Thus, I feel, it would be stupid to doubt the veracity of the document. Literally, everything capable of corroboration has been subsequently corroborated. As for the character and inclinations of the protagonist herself, I should count myself fortunate indeed to be able to corroborate that for myself!

Chapter Seven

(An unknown number of ms. pages missing)

. . . delight in my body. For Abdullah, though a cruel man and without doubt a criminal, was an imaginative lover.

The Godavari River was smooth, yellow, and oppressive. The nights were deep violent-blue, shadows everywhere, and the endless guttural din, low and suggestive of white-cloaked figures which squatted near the river, smoking to drive off the mosquitoes. Sometimes a voice was raised, a shout, drunken laughter, sometimes the shrill cry of a woman or the whine of skinny children, and often, merely the eternal croaking of the frogs in the thick yellowish silence.

'You will be my wife,' Abdullah had said, running his strong brown hand with its thick calloused fingers through his beard. 'You will have children. All the women have children. A woman is not a woman without children, and you will grow used to the life. We are an old people, a great people, although for the moment our star is not in the ascendant.'

He talked. Night after night when he returned to me he talked in a low guttural voice, indistinguishable from the voices of the other men, with the same heavy sensual accents, the same brave and wistful eyes. And his hand would come to rest on the hot sultry flesh of my thigh, and usually he would pull me underneath him and make love to me there and then, seeking I suspect to bind me to him by creating his child in me, a child of the river, brown, skinny, who, if he was not carried off by cholera or typhus or one of the other diseases, would grow up to be such a man, fearless, a rebel, who had never grown to accept the yoke which the English had through centuries of conquest foisted on his people.

I think he was proud to have conquered me, simply and childishly proud to have a white woman open her womb to his dark seed. And sometimes he would sit looking at me merely and softly call upon me to take off my clothes and bare the radiant smoothness of my torso for his dark and passionate lips.

From the beginning, of course, I had no intention of passing the remainder of my life there by the execrable stench of the Indian river. I would like to have borne his child for him, but I knew that that would be to seal my own fate. It was he whom I came near to loving, but with the love of a mature woman for her son. This great male who was the veritable king of the poor encampment on the banks of the Godavari was at heart a child, a child who rebelled against his 'father,' the British Raj, and who found in me a mother – a woman after all of the oppressors – who would connive and scheme with him for his eventual deliverance. Yes, I would not have grudged him a son, but to have become for always the subject of a subject and thus imperil my freedom so miraculously given back to me after the suicide flight over the Bay of Bengal – I could never have made that decision. Freedom? I don't know what that is, except that it has to do with the giving of the mystery of my flanks, with the taking of pleasure into myself; it is an act, but an act which must not be contaminated by an idealism such as Abdullah's, Abdullah the oppressed, Abdullah the rebel, Abdullah the liberator.

And so, one night I rose from our bed, rushes covered by a brightly coloured blanket, and made my way through the undergrowth to the dirt road which led to the main road, itself a dusty and ill-hewn highway, to Bombay. I experienced no exultation in my infidelity, but I moved on, nevertheless, and never thought once of returning.

Chapter Eight

The room is shuttered and hot. My companion is a girl of no more than fourteen, but in the fourteen days and nights during which we have been confined together she has grown from a slim young girl at the age of puberty into a plump little concubine whose startling whitish flesh, pale as mushrooms against her glossy black hair and the frail silken pubic hairs, hangs in pudgy rolls at her belly and thighs.

We are being groomed for love.

We are being fattened on a special enlarging diet of oil and semolina; closeted in obscurity, out of daylight, so that our soft flesh will acquire the oily plump whiteness of asparagus.

The room is shuttered and hot. We are unable to speak to one another, not knowing each other's language. For the first few days my companion merely stared at me, her eyes hostile, as though I were some strange and dangerous creature. Gradually, however, she ceased to be my enemy, and on the third day she ventured a shy and timid smile, and then, starved as we were of all other company and in the utter blackness of the fourth night as I lay at full length on the cushions which had been provided for me, I felt a sudden soft movement close at hand and the satin feel of hot flesh close to mine. A thrill of anticipation ran through me and in the comforting dark I cast off all modesty and moved over to meet the soft and tremulous front which was exposed to me. My arms encircled her. Our mouths met, shuddered in connection, and opened their secrets to one another, more furtive and yet more complete from being wordless. Then, in the hot and musky atmosphere, poignant with the nurtured flesh of two young females bred for sex, we closed with one another, wetly, softly, and with low, moaning shudders of fulfilment.

After that, I was not afraid to continue with my task of recording my adventures. My companion watched during those long days with a quizzical look, and then, when our strange and unappetizing food was brought to us, when she saw me move quickly to conceal the incriminating document, she smiled and nodded her dusky oval head in understanding. One day, when our servant had disappeared after bringing in our bowls of semolina, she went over to where I had hidden my diary, pointed, and put one now-plump finger to her sensual lips. I smiled at her and nodded. At that, she returned to me, slipped her arms about my shoulders, and kissed me passionately on the lips.

So I know I am safe. And I will write now, because I am anxious to complete my account so that, that done, I can sink into my new self, stripped of civilised refinements, and come to be as she is, my present lover, the plump little olive-skinned animal who, in the orchidaceous atmosphere at night, will fold her thighs about me without fear.

I had gone some five miles along the main road before dawn, which rose redly over the brackish countryside. I walked as swiftly as I could, still clad in the blue and gold sari which Abdullah had given me. If I looked out of place there on the Bombay road, it was not because I looked like a white woman – I did not – but because my sari was too fine to have belonged to a peasant woman, and my brocaded slippers were not made to be scuffed about on the public road. Had I wished to merge with my background, I should have worn a sari of white cotton perhaps, and my feet should have been naked and stained with dust and mud.

At the time, however, all this did not occur to me. I hoped soon to be given a lift in an ox-cart and calculated, for Abdullah had informed me that we were 250 miles from Bombay, that with luck I should reach my destination in a fortnight. I was not without money, for I had taken some of the rupees which Abdullah had stolen from the Englishmen he had ambushed seven days before. I remembered with a shudder his gory description of how he had halted them with a cry for alms and how, all unsuspecting, they had fallen victim to his terrible knife. Abdullah was an outlaw, brave and handsome, with a superb brown body on which the muscles rippled like burnished brass, but he did not kill for gain, for the pleasure he could derive from money quickly earned, but from his idealism, for revenge. Such a man, while he might be attractive to some, made little appeal to me, beyond, that is, the obvious beauty of his physique. The most I could feel for him was the kind of indulgent love that a mother feels for a silly and headstrong child.

As the sun rose over the rustling vegetation I was surprised by the musical horn of a motor car which urged me to move over to the side of the road. I was so surprised that the scarf fell off my head, revealing the flowing locks of my golden hair. At that the car, which had been about to pass, halted, raising dust under its white-walled tyres about five yards behind me. It was a Rolls Royce. The rear door at my side opened and a fat, almost white Indian in a white suit stepped onto the roadway. He regarded me with a smile for a moment and then, approaching me, said:

'You are going far?'

I smiled at him. 'As far as Bombay,' I said.

'My dear lady!' His plump face broke into a beaming smile. 'You were going to walk?'

'I have no other means of transport, sir,' I said.

'Then I insist, madam, that you allow me to drive you there. For that is my destination, and there is plenty of room in the car.'

'With great pleasure,' I said pleasantly and stepped into the roomy car as he held the door open for me.

When he had reseated himself, puffing, beside me, he patted me in a fatherly way on my knee and said charmingly:

'I shall not embarrass you, my dear, with questions as to how you came to be in such a predicament, miles even from the nearest village, and in your present attire. You may tell me what you wish, but if you would rather not say anything then I shall be quite content to accept your company for what it is, a gift from the gods!'

I thanked him with a smile.

He leaned forward, tapping with his fat knuckles on the glass partition. 'Drive on, Ahmed,' he said to the chauffeur.

When he heard that I had made no arrangements for a hotel, Mr Pamandari – for that was the name of my benefactor – insisted that I accept his hospitality at his own home, a gigantic villa a few miles from the centre of Bombay. He would like, he said, to introduce me to his daughter, a girl of eighteen whom he proposed sending in the near future to Europe, Paris to be exact, where she would enter a finishing school. She was a lonely girl, he said, his only child, and if I would care to stay with them for a few weeks he was certain that she would be delighted with my company. She was called Nadya, after her mother who had been a Russian. In some ways, he said, she was a very lucky girl, for she alone would inherit his great fortune when he died.

I can truthfully say that I had no conception of what real wealth was until I entered the home of this rich Parsee. His house, a vast snow-white edifice standing in a large private park, boasted two swimming pools, stables which included some of the finest thoroughbreds in India, tennis courts, and a vast array of hothouses which contained all varieties of orchids and other exotic plants. Two private helicopters stood beyond a line of plane trees at the extreme end of the lawn. The vast garden was cultivated immaculately by a corps of fifty gardeners, stable boys, and other retainers. As for the house itself, it contained an indoor swimming pool of black marble, a large library, and a veritable catacomb of reception rooms, lounges, dressing rooms and bedrooms, and one vast sun room completely draped in soft white silks. It was in this latter room that I first saw Nadya, a dark and beautifully proportioned girl of eighteen, her superbly subtle curves draped in turquoise Shantung silks, her slender, almost hazel-coloured arms holding a wonderful mauve and white orchid above her head where she lay, examining its sensual curves from under her long jet-black eyelashes. She was obviously bored. She was lying on her back on the white silk-covered divan, one knee exposed through the split in her turquoise gown.

'Nadya!' her father called eagerly. He obviously doted upon this only child.

Lazily, she turned her head and her beautiful sensuous face relaxed in a radiant smile.

'Father!' she said in a voice at once gentle and husky. 'How wonderful you are back at last! Look, isn't this a wonderful orchid?'

'Beautiful, you naughty child!' the father said in an adoring voice. 'You have been at my prize orchids again!' He turned to me. 'Nadya has a passion for orchids. I have told her not to pluck them, they die so soon that way.'

'Ah, but father,' she said in a sweet voice, 'I couldn't resist this one. Surely you don't grudge your own daughter one of your orchids?'

'They are all yours, Nadya darling,' her father said in a tone of happy resignation, and he moved towards the divan on which she was reclining and kissed her on the forehead.

'Whom have you brought to see me?' she said in a soft engaging voice.

Her father turned towards me.

'Come and meet my daughter, Helen.'

I moved forward. Her dark eyes flickered over the blue and gold sari which I was still wearing. Her first words were:

'That's not a very pretty sari, is it Daddy?' And then to me: 'I shall give you much more pretty clothes than that.'

Her father chuckled indulgently. 'She is such a generous child!' he said half-apologetically, and turning to his daughter again: 'This is Helen, Nadya. She is going to be our guest for a few weeks.'

'Oh, how lovely!' said Nadya delightedly, slipping on to her feet from the divan and kissing me on both cheeks. Her beautiful young body exuded a perfume of jasmine, warm from her pale dusky flesh. 'And she must have the room next to mine!' she said, turning to her happy father again. 'And I can give her all the clothes she wants!'

'Take her, then, child,' her father said gently. 'She is your guest. Your old papa is tired after the long journey. He must rest tonight. Take care of your guest, Nadya.'

With that, he shook hands with me and left us alone. When he had gone, Nadya took me by the hand and led me upstairs to the bedroom adjoining her own. 'I'll run your bath,' she said eagerly, and slipped into the adjoining bathroom. I hesitated long enough to take in my surroundings, a richly carpeted room hung with flame-red silks, and then, docile as a lamb, I followed Nadya into the bathroom. This latter room was an amazing sight. It was decorated in a flame-red colour to match the room to which it formed an ante-room, and the bath, in the shape of a deep shell, was large enough to hold four people. Nadya was bending over the edge, stirring the water about with her hand. As I entered she looked round with a flashing smile and said: 'Get undressed, Helen, I'll help you bathe!'

Again just as meekly as before – this wonderful nymph had, as I was subsequently to discover, a way of getting just what she wanted in life, which was not surprising considering her physical beauty and her vast wealth – I did as I was told, slipping the sari off my firm breasts, down over the shadowed rise of my haunches to a blue and gold heap at my feet. 'How beautiful you are!' Nadya said delightedly. 'Wherever did my father find you? I think you're the most beautiful person I've seen in my whole life!'

'You should look in the mirror,' I said drily.

'Oh I do! Do you? But it's not much fun looking at oneself. It's much nicer to look at someone else!'

I agreed with a smile.

'Why don't you undress and bathe with me,' I said.

'Oh, could I?'

'Of course!' I laughed. Her childish delight was infectious.

'Oh, I'd *love* to! Oh, how glad I am you came, Helen!'

'I'm glad to be here,' I said, and I felt that that at least was the truth. Somehow, my previous existence, with all its excitements, even at its peak – I suppose that was with poor Hawkes – seemed lacking in scope beside all this. Nadya had literally everything, and she was offering, for the moment at least, to share it with me. 'You'd better get undressed,' I added. 'You can't bathe with your clothes on.'

She giggled and in a trice she was naked beside me.

A dusky flush appeared on her cheeks as she felt my eyes move downwards over her figure, from the smooth column of her neck over her dark pink pouting nipples to the warm wall of her adorable and delicately whorled belly below which, at the junction of her dully sensual thighs, her mound, a shadowy undergrowth, thrust itself cheekily forward. She gazed down at herself under her alluring eyelashes and then, looking up at me again, she said tentatively:

'I'm not as beautiful as you are . . .'

I laughed.

'Of course you are,' I said. 'You're the most adorable creature I've ever seen!'

'Do you really think so?'

I couldn't resist opening my arms to her. Without hesitation she ran into them, pressing her firm young body against mine and crushing my lips against hers in a passionate embrace. Poor child! What a violent surge of unsatisfied sex mounted within her! No wonder she was happy to have me there! Her father, with more money than he would ever know what to do with, had given her everything except an outlet for her passion.

I ran my fingers over the smooth and trembling flesh of her buttocks. She moaned with pleasure and hid her face in my neck. But I had no intention of satisfying her there and then. Later there would be time for that. And so I pushed her away from me gently and held her beautiful longing torso at arms' length.

'Softly, you pretty girl,' I whispered. 'Let us bathe now, we shall have all the time in the world for that later.'

She obeyed immediately and threw one of her pretty long legs over the side of the bath to test the heat of the water. As she did so, I noticed that the poor child's sex was wet with passion. I almost pitied her, but desisted.

We sat in the water facing one another and tickling one another with our feet.

'Oh, Helen, I have never enjoyed myself so much!' she said, sinking dreamily back into the water.

'You lovely child!' I said. 'You have everything in the world you can possibly want!'

'I have now!' she said contentedly.

I laughed.

'You silly girl, you want a man, not me!'

She chuckled. 'Helen,' she said, 'have you ever made love with a man?'

'I did once,' I said with a smile.

'What was it like?' Her question rang out like a pistol shot.

'You little bitch in heat!' I exclaimed.

She pouted.

'It's alright for you!' she said stubbornly. 'You've slept with a man. I've hardly even *seen* one except for my father.'

'Your father is protecting you,' I said.

'Oh, I know all that! That's what he says! I just wish he would forget to protect me one day!'

'Never mind, Nadya,' I said. 'I'll tell you about it and one day you'll have a man too.'

'Will you, Helen?' She half-swam through the water towards me. 'Kiss me like a man does!' she said.

I took her beautiful head between my hands and kissed her long and passionately on the mouth, forcing her lips apart with my tongue and sliding the latter into her mouth. She breathed heavily, her beautifully-formed breasts tilted and tightening in passion, and sucked softly and contentedly at my proffered passion. But I drew away from her.

'That's how a man kisses,' I said.

'It's wonderful!' she exclaimed. 'Can we do it often, Helen?'

'I intend to get washed now,' I said firmly. 'I've travelled a long way and I'm hot and sticky.'

'Oh, I'm sorry!' she said, suddenly repentant. 'What a beast I am not letting you have your bath in peace! But I like you so much, Helen. You will stay for a long time, won't you?'

'If you want me,' I said.

'I want you more than anything else in the world!' she said extravagantly.

'Except a man,' I said drily, and began to soap my arms.

Nadya's bedroom opened onto a broad balcony. There, by the silver light which was shed through the open windows of the bedroom, we took dinner together, looking out across the great park. The night air was soft and scented with exotic vegetation brought from all corners of the globe to be transplanted in this haven of a loved daughter's girlhood, and these natural scents, of the flowers, exhalations of the budding trees, blended subtly with the delicate aromas distilled in the perfumeries of Arabia and France which clung to our bathed and silk-draped limbs. The room behind us glittered with silver and gold cloth and projected a suffusion of enchanted light over the delicacies which lay on the table before us. Faint night-noises came to us across the park.

'What's that light over there?' I asked Nadya.

'It's the headlights of a car on the road about a mile away,' Nadya replied sweetly. 'Sometimes I watch them for hours,' she sighed. 'They are all going somewhere. I never go anywhere. The park is lovely but it's a bore.'

'Your father said that he was going to send you to school in Paris,' I said. 'Do you not know about it?'

She smiled wistfully. 'He would never send me without a chaperone. He might say he is going to but he never will. My mother wanted it. My mother was a beautiful woman, a woman of the world. My father is in some ways very provincial. My mother used to laugh at him.'

'I'll speak to him, Nadya. I'll tell him it would be good for you to go to France.'

'Oh, if you will, he may listen to you!'

'The only point is, Nadya, that the reason you want to go is precisely the reason he *doesn't* want you to go.'

She laughed softly.

'You don't need to tell him that,' she said slyly.

'Do you think he doesn't know?'

'Oh, dear!' she said in the voice of a spoilt child. 'I'll never get away!' And then she became suddenly excited. 'Listen, Helen! If you were to offer to go with me to Europe, he might let me go!'

'Don't be silly, I hardly know him.'

'Oh, but he likes you, I can tell. He might let me go if you were to go with me – really, Helen. You'd like to go, wouldn't you?'

It was a possibility. The only trouble was that I didn't have a passport. My journey halfway around the world was illegal. I wondered whether Mr Pamandari could get me one. Ever since I had set out from Australia, my steps had been dogged by the lack of this vital document. At any moment if the police should question me I could be in trouble. But surely my host, with all his vast wealth, could arrange to get one for me? And Nadya's father would surely do his utmost if his daughter begged him to. I decided to tackle Nadya on the subject that very night. I had no doubt that she would be a willing accomplice.

'You would like to go, wouldn't you?' she said again.

'Yes, Nadya, but let's not talk about it just now. Later, when we go to bed.'

A crafty look came over the girl's beautiful face. 'You will sleep with me,' she announced. And then she giggled. 'It will be fun, won't it?'

'What would your father say?'

'Oh, he'll never know! We'll rumple up your bed as though you'd slept in it and we'll lock both our doors. Anyway, there's a communicating door between our rooms. If anybody comes, you can easily slip back to your own bed before I open the door. See, it's easy!'

I laughed resignedly.

'Alright,' I said. 'But only for tonight.'

She giggled again. 'Oh, Helen, you're wonderful! Let's go soon, now! Wait! I must go and say goodnight to Papa. I'll tell him you were tired after the journey and have gone to bed.' With that, she rose from her seat on the balcony and ran into the room towards the door. As I heard it close behind her, I got up myself and walked slowly across Nadya's room to the communicating door. In my own room I turned down the bed and undressed, and then, wearing a thin silk nightgown, I slipped back into Nadya's room, climbed into her bed, and drew the covers up to my chin. With Nadya's help, I had begun to realise, nothing was beyond me.

Her silvery laugh came from the other side of the room.

'Helen! You're in bed already!' She was standing with her back to the door, which she had locked behind her, slim, of medium height, as graceful as a fawn. Her dark eyes were shining delightedly in my direction, and then, suddenly meek, she hung her head and moved across the room silently towards me.

'I said goodnight to Papa,' she said, sitting down at the edge of the bed, almost reluctant, I felt, to remove her clothes.

I watched her with a smile.

'Shall I come in now?' It was the voice of a child.

'You'd better take your clothes off first,' I said.

Once again, in a lightning movement, she peeled her sensuous flesh of its silk coverings and stood naked before me. Again, ashamed of her body's heat, her petal-like eyelids drooped, veiling the eagerness of the dark eyes. Her movements were beautiful. When she poised on the balls of her feet, her pelvis was thrust forward and her breasts pricked into firm erection. Her full buttocks and her delicately studded belly shone dully with that peculiar gloss of young and virgin flesh, while the proud black tussock at the crux of her torso overhung the smooth and supple downward sweep of her tapering legs. With hesitation, she opened her eyes and looked down at me. 'Do you really think I'm beautiful, Helen?'

'Of course you are!'

'I'm coming in,' she said, as though to conceal her nervousness. I did not reply. A moment later, in the darkness – for with nervous haste she moved over quickly and switched out the light – I felt her desperate young flesh close against me. I took her firmly and gently into my arms. She made no resistance, shuddered slightly and buried her face in my neck. With one hand I touched her buttocks, grazing their delicate skin with slow titillating strokes to kindle her hymeneal torch with the flint of desire. She breathed deeply and her body exuded a sweat as delicate and as tentative as spring rain. 'Kiss me like a man, Helen,' she whispered urgently. I moistened my lips with my tongue and lifted her head so that hers, dry with fearful anticipation, waited at a distance of a fraction of an inch, a leaf's thickness away, and slightly apart, inviting like the curtains of a woman who is desperate but ashamed. I touched their soft palpable surface with the tip of my tongue, moistening the contours and causing her whole torso to twitch and quiver. Then my lips pressed more firmly against hers, her resistance gave, and my tongue penetrated into the melting vortex of her mouth. At first it was slack, passive, and unresponsive. It was the torrid part of her body which responded, blindly, closing its simmering flesh against me in the strange tropical heat generated by our bodies beneath the sheets. The mouth, which I suppose she identified with her will, for it was her mouth which was being wooed, or thus anyway she deceived herself, was open in a soft desperate paralysis. She would not give. She was being taken. She ignored the ebullient purpose of her loins, the feverish volcano which, set like a second and less modest mouth at the junction of her sweltering thighs, rubbed itself voluptuously like a cat against my thigh. That mouth was out of sight and thus she could pretend that it did not exist. Its luxury, its dissipation, was no part of her will which, mummified little nothing that it was, sought to give the impression of resistance by a feigned passivity of lips and tongue, which was the more sensitive under the sham anaesthetic. Shortly, however, even the show of resistance became impossible. She could delude herself no longer. She wanted me to goose her, to pretend that I was the man whom, in the lonely meadow of her bed, she had desired since the age of puberty. Tentatively, I felt her lips close round my tongue, making a voluptuous channel for it, shadowing in time, in imagination, the channel which she would gladly give to the male thing when it would come. Softly, through our gentle lipping motions, her whispered words came to me: 'Be a man for me, Helen!' All this while, I had not been physically insensible. The vast liquefaction of my ever-present desire had already spread throughout the soft vinery of my limbs. I could no longer resist the child's passion. My fingers sought her soft and excited crevice, pruning the hairs, and slipping easily at first into the wonderful slime-coated sheath. She was a virgin. How ludicrous for this beautiful creature to have suffered so long! I would have given anything at that moment to be a man. As it was, there was something abortive in this sweet cultivation of her. How soft she was against the fine linen sheet! What a weight of sensuality quivered in her bossy thighs! What superb husbandry the tillage of this virgin field demanded! I felt suddenly unworthy, remembering the day of my own spring and my bucolic capers on the lonely beach. My first lover had been the sea himself, Poseidon, ravishing me under a wave. But it was too late to back out now. The subtle grammar of her sex had transformed this peerless Indian maiden into a lusty wench such as one might find giving herself to an elderly ploughman in the hayloft of a barn. She was a slut, a hot bitch who demanded satisfaction. She no longer spoke or even attempted to. She was a sweet bitch in the raw, gamey, sweaty, sweltering, bucking her beautiful arse like a serving-maid under a milkman. She intended to be had and my slender fingers were already too far in for safety. Her maidenhead was rending. Her whole belly was in flames. 'A . . . aaa . . . eee . . .' This had the effect of putting me at a distance. I felt responsible for her. If her father found out he would skin me alive and I had already realised that the morrow's sheets would bear the telltale marks. I shook her and tried to bring her to her senses.

'Nadya!' I said urgently, removing my fingers hastily. I felt myself grasped desperately and her body, suffocated with its passion, used mine as I had used the log on the beach a long time ago. But I was adamant. If this was what she wanted she would have it. But I had no intention of compromising my position as a friend of the family. I took her cruelly by the neck and with my knee I forced her smouldering loins away from me. But I had reckoned without the will of the child. That factor in the situation had now reversed its direction and was reinforcing the white-hot combustive lust which had incendiarised her whole belly.

She had gone mad. 'Do it!' she said fiercely. 'If you don't do it, I'll scream and tell my father you forced me!'

Nothing would extinguish her. At least nothing which seemed to go against her will. And so I changed my tactics.

'Nadya, darling,' I crooned. 'Of course I am going to do it to you! I want to do it as much as you do! But we must be careful my little virgin! Otherwise the servants will know and it may get to your father . . . you wouldn't want that, would you?'

This had the effect of calming her. Her grip relaxed.

'How?' she said.

'We must turn on the light for a moment,' I said. 'Do it and I'll show you.'

There was no shyness in her movements. Her smouldering young body was brought into bold relief by the soft electric lights. She stood there, a few yards from the bed, her wonderful tawny breast heaving and her belly rising and falling with the effort of breathing.

I slipped out of the bed and turned back the sheets. There, on the snow-white linen was a tell-tale stain of blood.

She looked at it with non-comprehension.

'Is that me?' she asked in a small voice.

'Yes, darling,' I said. 'That's what I mean. We must be careful.'

Quickly I removed the sheet and carried it into Nadya's bathroom. She followed me like a little dog and stood watching me with interest. As I rinsed the stained part of the sheet in cold water I was suddenly struck by our twin reflection in the mirror. I was fair and she was dark. Without exaggeration I don't think I had ever seen two such superb young creatures. Both bodies seem to be inhabited by an almost supernatural lissome radiance. There was not an ugly curve on either of us.

My tenderness for her returned.

'You see, darling,' I said. 'You haven't done this before. And the first time one does it one always bleeds a little. It's nothing to worry about, but we must take precautions.' I wrung the water out of the sheet and examined it to see if any traces of the mark remained.

Nadya, meanwhile, nodded, came close to me, and kissed me lightly on the cheek. 'You're very good to me, Helen. I didn't mean it about telling my father, honestly I didn't!'

I smiled. At the time she would have screamed without compunction. She was used to having her own way and would make a bad enemy.

'Of course not, darling,' I said gently. 'But if you want to go on, we must take precautions.'

'Oh, we *must* go on, Helen! I've never experienced anything like it in my whole life! Please let's go on, Helen!'

'Alright, but you must promise to do as I tell you. If you disobey your husband as you tried to disobey me, he'll beat you.'

'He wouldn't dare!' she said proudly, but then her air of superiority was suddenly transformed into a look of genuine surprise. 'Would he, Helen?'

'You wait and see,' I said. 'But meanwhile, if you do as you're told, you'll never have cause to complain that your Helen wasn't good to you.'

'Oh, I'll be good, Helen! I promise I will! And I'll tell you what! I'll get my father to get you everything you want!'

'There is something I want, as a matter of fact,' I said, 'but we'll speak about that later.'

'Oh, what is it, Helen? Tell me and I'll get it for you!'

'You wouldn't understand. It's a passport.'

'What's that?'

'Don't worry your pretty little head about it. I'll speak to your father about it.'

'Come on, Helen . . .' She had forgotten about it already. She was standing close to me, her hands on my naked hips, with a playful sensual smile on her lips.

'Just be patient, Nadya. Here, take this sheet and put it back on the bed. I've got to find something to put over it.'

She took it gaily and slipped back into the bedroom.

When she had gone, I selected a large bath towel. She had laid the sheet on the bed again and was lying naked on top of it, her arms stretched out like a cross and her legs spread wide, like the estuary of a deep river. I couldn't withhold my admiration. 'Really, Nadya,' I said, 'you're the loveliest girl I've ever seen!'

She smiled, simulating shyness.

'What would you like to do to me?' Her voice was sensual.

'You'll find out soon enough,' I said, advancing towards the bed. I threw the towel towards her. 'Put that underneath you on top of the sheet,' I said.

She obeyed.

A moment later I was in bed with her.

Her soft hands, still moist, alighted at once on my hips and drew the lower part of my body towards her. At the same time I was surprised to feel her fingers, restless and inquisitive, like birds at a nest. 'Do you like that?' she whispered softly. In answer I put my arms round her and drew her close to me, forging close, and our lips met again, this time without hesitation and completely thawed in sexual abandon. Meanwhile, the corrosive motion of her fingers ignited the seed, as incandescent as magnesium, in my loins, and, chafing strongly with my limbs, I swung one heavy thigh across her and mounted her. She trembled at my weight, dragged her legs from under me and raised them in a cleft stick on either side. She had asked for it and I intended to give her it without mercy. I felt my hands take hold of her. A low quavering whinny burst from her lips and her long nails sank into the flesh at my shoulderblades. I let her body grow used to the feel of the thing inside her and then I began to strum her, *diminuendo*, until her magnetized hips rose and fell in a strange syncopated dance. She came soon after that, for the first time in her life, and in the heat of her virginity. As her body's movements grew slack, I drew her buttocks on to my shoulders, and pressed my mouth against her lovely wound. Her belly rose and fell, expiring, so it seemed, all the waters of her maidenhood. Her belly was wet with the delicate perfumed perspiration of her quenched lust. Under my tonguing, however, her passion began to reassert itself. I caught it in its rise, reversed positions, and forced her head to my own soft lyre. She fell to her task with an eagerness which soon brought the sacred fire into the most Stygian, the most crepuscular part of me.

'I see, 'Mr Pamandari said. 'Well, don't worry my dear, it can no doubt be arranged.'

We were seated in the sun room, Nadya, her father, and myself. It was about a week after my arrival. During that week Nadya and I had become inseparable. She had brought up the subject and Mr Pamandari had turned to me in a fatherly way and asked me how I happened to be in India without a passport. Briefly, omitting all compromising details, I told him of my leaving home and of my stowing away on a merchant ship which was bound for India. I admitted that I had been discovered in the hold but said that I had managed to leave the ship, unknown to the Captain, at Madras. From there on, I told him I had wandered through India until the moment at which he had found me near the Godavari River. He was kind enough not to insist on details. On the contrary, whenever I seemed embarrassed in my account, he glossed over the subject with a 'Yes, of course, it's not important,' until, when I had finished, he said,

'I see,' patted me on the shoulder, and told me not to worry about it.

'It may be difficult,' he continued, 'to obtain a British passport. There, it is not easy to bribe. But I can no doubt get you a Turkish passport, or an Egyptian one. We shall see.'

Nadya jumped up and kissed her father on the forehead. 'I told her you would get one for her and you will, won't you?'

'I shall do my best, dear,' said the Parsee modestly, and added, 'if I would do it for Helen alone, then you may be sure that if it is your wish also I shall be doubly certain to do it.'

'There!' said Nadya, turning to me triumphantly.

Mr Pamandari waved aside my attempt to thank him.

'My dear,' he said, 'if you could for one moment imagine the change you have wrought in Nadya since your fortunate arrival in this house, you would realise that it is I who am indebted to you. You have been more than a sister to her. So say no more about it.'

'Papa,' Nadya said, 'if Helen would come to Europe with me, would you allow me to go?'

'Haha!' he said with an indulgent smile. 'So that is why you are so anxious for Helen to have a passport!'

'Well, it's one of the reasons,' Nadya admitted grudgingly.

'And how do you feel about it, Helen?' he said, turning to me.

When I shrugged my shoulders in an effort to seem constrained, he continued:

'One of the reasons I have not allowed Nadya to go to Europe has been the fact that I knew of no one in whose charge I could send her. As you know, my daughter will one day be a very rich young lady. Naturally, I am not happy about the thought that without proper supervision she may fall for the charms of some mountebank. But this puts a different complexion on the matter.

If you were willing to escort her during her sojourn, I might not feel so bad about it. Nadya knows nothing about the world. To some extent, that is my fault. But then, it is always difficult for a widower like myself. Whom should I trust? She has no mother, no sisters. But now it is different. I have seen her bloom in your company. And I flatter myself that I am a shrewd enough judge of character to know that you, Helen, are to be trusted implicity. You would see to it that she didn't get into bad company. I have never been in Paris myself, but they tell me that it is a sink of vice. And if one can judge from the literature that comes out of that city I am inclined to believe it. Virginity there is evidently not worth a fig!'

I had my doubts if virginity was worth a fig anywhere, more doubts about whether it ought to be, but I refrained from expressing them. I said merely:

'My dear Mr Pamandari, I am deeply grateful for your opinion of me, all the more so because I am not worthy of it. I suspect that any young person would have made your daughter happy. She has been too much alone for too long a time. Of course she is glad to have company, but to be her protector in a foreign country, really, I doubt whether I could undertake such a responsibility.'

This pretty speech redoubled his trust in me. He actually got up from his chair and kissed my hand.

'Dear Helen,' he said, 'it is because you would not lightly undertake such a responsibility that I have faith in you. Oh, you must forgive me! But I have not been blind to your devotion to my daughter since you came to my house. You have been both a mother and a sister to her!'

And a husband, I said under my breath.

'I would have to think it over,' I said at length.

'Do so, dear lady! And rest assured that should you decide to accompany her, there will be adequate means at your disposal to make the trip just as enjoyable as you would want it to be. But think it over, by all means, for I am in no hurry to get rid of either of you!'

Chapter Nine

We have been here for three weeks. No male has been to see us during all this time. But from the mood of my companion I suspect that our time here is drawing to a close. Every time the servant enters with our bowls of semolina the girl giggles. She is obviously expecting a visit from someone else. She grows more excited daily. She is now a little barrel of soft whitish flesh, tufted voluptuously at its centre.

For myself, I too have put on weight, but, being taller, the fat which I have put on – it is most evident at my thighs, my belly, and at the front of my body close to my armpits – is not, even from a western point of view, so unbecoming. I can understand a man's preferring the opaque weight of flesh as it has been cultivated on us. From my point of view, it makes little or no difference. On the contrary, if, in the eyes of the men I shall eventually meet, it increases my desirability, my attraction as a sexual object, then it is all for the good; I welcome my new condition.

But I am certainly looking forward to the end of this strange imprisonment. I am bored by this girl. She giggles all the time. I suspect she has been bought from a poor family, that in the past she had to work, and that she is more than content to have put that life behind her for the sluggish luxury of the present one.

Because of the diet, perhaps, I have become lethargic. I have no wish to do anything. When the time comes, I shall be quite content to love and sleep — a torporous round — I think I was born to be one of the lotus-eaters. In the west everybody is busy because his neighbour is. Mountains of industry, seas of commerce come into being, and, once in being, exert their damning influence on the sons and grandsons of those who created them. Art, the aesthetic of the flesh, the cultivation of leisure, are despised, tolerated, perhaps, but basically thought of as not quite respectable. Love in the west thus becomes hysterical, almost epileptic. Everything is computed in terms of time, so much time for this, so much time for that; it must not be 'wasted.' Geared for industry, those stupid westerners never pause to analyse the word 'waste.' Time is accepted without question as valuable; like money or land or food, it must not be 'wasted'; at the end of an hour one must have something to show for it. The question for them is: What 'excuse' for passing the hour in such and such a way? If one can produce riches at the end of the hour, then the time has not been 'wasted.' But if one has merely derived pleasure from living? If one considers living important — in itself?

The western God, the Jewish God, was invented to make the hatred of life logical.

We sailed in the most luxurious suite of the new luxury liner, the *Empress of Nepal*.

Mr Pamandari had provided me with a cheque book.

'Write cheques as you require them, my dear,' he had said with an indulgent smile. 'Spend liberally and do not try to economise. All I ask is that you look after Nadya's interests. Keep her out of trouble.'

He waved to us from the pierhead as the huge liner, on its maiden cruise, was pulled slowly out of the harbour by an army of tugs. When his stout friendly figure disappeared in the distance we went immediately to our suite and began to unpack our luggage.

We had both been provided with an elaborate trousseau which contained a complete European outfit, costumes, dresses for morning, afternoon, and evening, as well as an indescribable variety of Indian costumes. Two maids accompanied us and did the actual work of the unpacking under our directions. Their names were Sarah and Luna, pretty, delightful creatures with large black eyes and a zest for life. They could hardly contain their excitement about the trip, and when they passed from one room to another in each other's company we would hear their excited tinkling laughter coming through the open door.

Nadya sighed with pleasure and threw herself on a chaise longue. 'Helen,' she said, 'do you think Sarah and Luna do what we do? I mean, do servants do that as well?'

'Of course,' I replied. I was filing my nails.

'I'm not sure that I like it,' she said.

'What?'

'Their doing it.'

I looked up from my hand.

'Why on earth shouldn't they?'

She pouted. 'Well, they're only servants after all . . .'

'They're human.'

'Oh, I suppose so,' she admitted grudgingly. 'But, Helen, you don't suppose a man would prefer them to us, do you?'

'*Some* men might. It all depends on the man.'

She didn't appear to be very pleased about this. After a moment she said: 'Well, whenever we go anywhere we'll leave them at home, won't we?'

'Of course. You don't take your servant everywhere.'

'Oh, I'm glad about that, because Helen . . .' She was looking at me with great seriousness.

'Yes?'

'When mother was alive, she had a maid called Tajli – it's a pretty name, isn't it?—and one day I heard my mother quarrelling with my father. She was saying she couldn't bear the thought of him with a servant. I didn't know what she meant at the time.'

'And what did your father say?'

'Papa just laughed. Laughed! How horrible for my mother! And he said that if she liked she could get another maid. And she said: 'So that you can spend more time with that horrible little Tajli!' And he said he didn't see that it mattered whether it was Tajli or someone else, that at least you could control a servant. But my mother said that it was unbearable. I remember her words, 'Quite unbearable!' she said. And so Tajli went away.'

'Your mother was a European.'

'I think she was quite right,' said Nadya with emphasis. 'Sarah and Luna had better not try to interfere with my men!'

'I'm sure they'll be too busy with their own,' I said.

'Well, I hope so.'

There was evidently no doubt in Nadya's mind as to the object of her trip. She was out to have a man, and the sooner the better. And, as I realised that I would be quite unable to prevent her, I took the opportunity of instructing her in the art of birth control. I had no mind to have her pregnant by the first oaf who happened to conceive a lust for her. While I did not sympathise with her father's views on virginity, I had every respect for his fears regarding her enslavement by a mountebank. Without me, she would have been the dupe of the first handsome gold-digger who came along. When I considered this, I began to have doubts about the supposed naiveté of Mr Pamandari. It was just possible that he recognised the inutility of starving his daughter any longer, and recognising in me a woman of the world, he had decided that under the circumstances I was the best possible 'chaperone' for her. After all, he was old and experienced enough to know that only a poor woman is compromised by a bad reputation. A girl of Nadya's beauty and wealth is above being compromised unless she gives all her money away to some scoundrel. And Nadya was unable to do this for the simple reason that only I could write the cheques and only Mr Pamandari could honour them. I was so struck by the wisdom of this scheme that I went straight to the Radio Office and sent the following cable to my benefactor:

Don't worry about Nadya. She will return in one piece and without attachments.

Love, Helen.

Two hours later I received the following reply:

Trust you implicitly. Have always respected intelligence.

Love, Pamandari.

I felt very happy about this discovery. I had hitherto believed that I would have to keep up a pretence of virtue in front of Nadya's father. Now it was a relief to know that barring strangleholds there were no fouls in this exciting game. Nadya could 'wrestle' to her 'heart's' content; I was on hand to see that she didn't get her neck broken.

I decided at once that as soon as we had had dinner (which was served to us in the dining room of our own suite) we would scout out the territory in the ballroom on the first-class deck. When I suggested this to Nadya, she was delighted. It would be the first time that she had been let loose amongst men.

Thus, a few hours later, immaculately clad in the most expensive of evening dresses, we entered the ballroom. It was already crowded with excited men and women – the usual miscellaneous group one finds on the first-class deck of a luxury liner, some there for pleasure, others for profit, all without exception excited by the prospects which membership of a completely new and cosmopolitan society afloat on the ocean offered them. There would, I supposed, be few virgins at the end of the voyage. With that thought at the forefront of my mind, I steered the beautiful Nadya across to the bar. As we crossed the floor I was conscious of all eyes turning in our direction. This was hardly surprising. A ship is a small world. Our fellow passengers would no doubt be aware that it was we who occupied the so-called 'Royal Suite' on board the *Empress of Nepal*. They would also be aware that we were travelling alone with two maids and otherwise unchaperoned. Add to this the fact that we were without doubt the two best-looking young women aboard and it is not difficult to understand why we attracted attention. The mothers of virgins were jealous of us, the eligible young men were inquisitive about us, and the sharks converged upon us. At least three men of various ages made their way discreetly towards the bar in front of us.

Before we reached the bar, however, one of the ship's officers had advanced and presented each of us with a large bouquet of roses, this service doubtless arranged for by the machinations of Mr Pamandari of Bombay. We accepted them casually and continued to the bar, where the crowd made way for us and soon we were seated on two of the high barstools, our pretty high heels just visible below the hems of our dresses.

The barman bowed. 'Miss Pamandari, Miss Seferis,' he said with a smile of greeting.

I must explain that the passport which Nadya's father had obtained for me was a Greek one, and my name was now Helen Seferis.

We took coffee and liqueurs. As Joe, the barman, was filling our glasses, a bronzed young man of about thirty, coming up from Nadya's side, spoke to us.

'May I introduce myself?' he said in a pleasant American voice. 'My name's Devlin, Harry Devlin. I'm from Boston.'

'Oh,' said Nadya sweetly, 'where's that?'

Mr Devlin appeared to be slightly put out by this innocent question. But he retained his smile, saying, 'It's in Massachusetts, you know – I'm from New England.'

'My father knows many Englishmen,' Nadya said pleasantly.

'Mr Devlin means he's an American,' I said helpfully.

'Yeah, that's right,' Mr Devlin said.

'I am Nadya Pamandari,' Nadya said. 'And this is my friend Helen Seferis.'

'Glad to know you, Miss Seferis,' Mr Devlin said.

After finishing our drinks we retired to one of the tables in the ballroom with the young man whose modest conversation and handsome figure made a great impression on Nadya. She danced a number of dances with him. Meanwhile, a second young man had joined us. He was an Italian called Mario Ratsonli. He was, if anything, a little younger than Harry Devlin, and very good looking in a Latin way. He seemed to prefer me to Nadya, and, as we danced he had a delicious habit of placing one of his thighs between mine so that through two or three thicknesses of material I could feel the shape of his strong thigh on my mound.

I did nothing to discourage his obvious advances, nestling close with my belly against his as we danced round the room. Only when he suggested that we should go out on the deck together did I think it necessary temporarily to call a halt.

'Later, Mario,' I said with a smile. 'For the moment I would rather dance.'

He followed me meekly back to the table where Nadya and

Harry Devlin were already seated. As we sat down, Nadya said excitedly:

'Harry's been telling me all about America, Helen! It must be a wonderful place! Perhaps Papa would let us go there after we've been to Paris.'

Devlin was obviously flattered by the unembarrassed attentions of this beautiful young Indian girl. Looking him over, I decided that she could have done worse for her first experiment. He was handsome, generous, obviously not poor as I suspected Mario was; indeed, at that moment I had no doubts about him. Devlin danced with me next and during the dance took none of the liberties which Mario had taken.

'You're a friend of the family?' Devlin said in an obvious attempt to place me.

'Hardly,' I said. 'Mr Pamandari is a business associate of my father.' I said this because I thought it would be unwise to have it known that I was Nadya's watch-dog. Few people know anything about Greece, so I might have been anyone's daughter.

The change in his attitude was obvious. He took much more care with his dancing and ushered me to my seat as though I were something of more than ordinary fragility.

I had already made up my mind to sleep with Mario and decided to take the first opportunity to tell Nadya that she had my approval if she felt like sleeping with Devlin. There were four or five bedrooms attached to our suite and so, with a certain amount of discretion, it would be quite possible to provide opportunities for both men. For this reason, I took Nayda's arm and led her through into the retiring room. I told her of my plan, warned her again to take the precautions I had outlined to her, and told her that I would leave with Mario after the next dance.

'Wait at least half an hour,' I said, 'because we may stroll around the deck for a while. And see that Devlin leaves before dawn.'

After that we powdered our noses, kissed one another, and returned to the ballroom.

Mario danced even more sensually than before.

His hand sometimes strayed from my waist to the naked part of my back, and the touch of his fingers combined with the intertwining movement of our lower bodies lulled me into an apposite sensuality. We were turning slowly near the exit.

'Let's go on deck for a while,' I said suddenly.

He agreed with alacrity and as we went out I had a last glimpse of Nadya and Devlin. They were leaning towards one another over the table, he fingering his champagne glass, and she looking into his eyes, talking like conspirators. I felt a slight pressure at my arm and followed Mario onto the deck.

For a while we stood looking over the rail, looking down at the streaming beads of efflorescence, glowing like phosphorus, which bounded from the belly of the ship and disappeared along the side into our wake. Mario dropped his cigarette end, which fell in an apparently curving line to the sea.

I yawned. 'I'm tired,' I said. 'I don't think I'll go back to the dance. It's so stuffy in there.'

He followed politely as I made my way towards our suite, and as I put out my hand to say goodnight I wondered what excuse he was going to make to follow me in. He accepted my hand but held it in his own without letting go. 'Are you not going to invite me in to take a nightcap?' he said.

'Just for a moment, then,' I said, 'because I'm very tired.'

He followed me in to the sitting room.

'Make yourself comfortable,' I said. 'What will you have?'

'You have cognac?'

I poured two large cognacs and carried one over to him. Then

I sat down beside him on the couch. For a few minutes we sat making small talk and then I rose, switched on the radiogram, and returned to my seat. I turned down the lights, leaving only one lamp which cast a pale circular ring on the carpet near our feet.

'Let's dance,' I said.

He got to his feet immediately and took me in his arms. It was a slow foxtrot. We glided silently out of range of the lamp, our bodies pressed close together and moving voluptuously in unison. Once again I felt his thigh insistent between mine and his hand slipped downwards from my waist onto the soft rise of the material at my buttocks. We swayed together, all motion of our feet suspended, until gradually, like the pendulum of a clock which has run down, our oscillations grew slighter until they were negligible, a slightly tremorous fluctuation, the lower part of our bodies set firmly together, and his handsome face hovered above mine in the semidarkness, his dark eyes smiling and his soft lips approaching mine. And then there was only the music, the slow sensual voice of the crooner coming to us across the dark room. 'It's better with our clothes off,' he whispered. I laughed softly in his face and led him into one of the bedrooms.

We didn't turn on the light. The music soft now, in the distance. I removed his tie and then stepped back to undress myself. I took off everything except the dark nylon stockings and my high-heeled shoes and then stepped back against his naked body. His sex rode up towards my navel and our thighs mingled with the softness of velvet. We were still dancing when the music stopped. We paused, almost without moving, to wait for it to begin, our bellies rising and falling against one another, quivering at the delicate peeling contact like aspen leaves. I laid my blonde head on his shoulder. His strong hands explored all my skin surfaces tenderly. And then he tilted my face upwards towards him and kissed me, at the same time forcing me back, my torso curved and springy as a longbow, against the bed. Its soft horizontal bulk caught me exactly at the bend of my knees and, off balance, I crumpled giddily backwards, drawing his hot hard body on top of me.

At that moment, the music began again. But it came to us from a distance, and only intermittently, seeping into the air about us, to be sucked into our consciousness of the situation only at those instants at which our sexual gyration hung fire, slewed into relief, shadowy flesh transfixed for an instant in time, and hushed voices on the deck outside, to merge with a suggestive bar of music, urgently, as we whirlpooled down again to become the minute electric ebb and flow which caused waves of sexual hunger to pass through our quivering flanks and in the end caused such delectable devastation at our loins. There was something massive about that act of love. Its force was tidal. The small seismic disturbance in the hollow of my belly increased to the force of an avalanche. It transmitted itself to every sinew and reigned there like an all-embracing quake, sweet and needling at its depth, until every belly and buttock muscle of my big girl's body, all the gimbals of my flesh, creaked, broke, and cracked in delirious pain, indefinitely shadowed by a movement as vast as that of shifting continents.

Suddenly, in the next room, I heard Nadya laugh softly, and then Devlin's voice like the voice of a conspirator. I reached up the bed with my hand, turned down the soft sheet, and with a soft persuasive movement of my body encouraged Mario to follow me into it.

Shortly afterwards, another door in the suite closed. As my new lover mounted me again, I thought of Nadya's young body knowing a male for the first time.

*   *   *

'Aren't men wonderful?' Nadya said at breakfast.

'Are you sure you were careful, darling?'

She pouted. 'Of course I was! Anyone would think I was a child!'

I smiled. 'I just don't want you to have any trouble, that's all.'

'I don't see that it would matter, anyway!' she said rebelliously. 'I'd love to have Harry's child!'

'Oh, you would, you little bitch!' I said sweetly. 'And what would your father say?'

'Well,' she said, 'Harry and I could get married, and then Papa would be a grandfather and he'd like Harry too, I know.'

'Is that what Harry said?' I asked drily.

'Well, he told me he loved me.'

'That is quite immaterial to me,' I said sharply. 'Did he say he wanted to marry you?'

'Of course it's too early to tell,' Nadya said brightly. 'But he hinted at it.'

'Ughuh,' I said gently, 'I think I'd better speak to Mr Devlin.'

'You will not! I'll never speak to you again if you do!'

'You will do just as you're told, my pet,' I said calmly. 'Otherwise, I'll send you straight back to India.'

'You wouldn't dare! You couldn't!' Her lovely features were contorted in anger.

'Listen, Nadya,' I said softly. 'You can sleep with Harry Devlin to your heart's content, but I don't want to hear one word about marriage. Do you understand?'

'Anyone would think he was a leper!'

'As far as marriage is concerned, he is.'

'What have you got against him? Anyone would think you wanted him for yourself!'

'Think that if you want,' I said coolly, 'but if you make one move towards marriage, I'll take him away from you. Do you understand?'

'You couldn't!'

She said it desperately, unable to conceal the fear in her voice.

'Eat your breakfast, darling,' I said. 'Why can't you be sensible? There are a million better men than Harry in this world.'

'You're just jealous!' she fired back, and rising abruptly, she threw open the door and went out on deck.

Trouble already. That is the difficulty about men like Harry Devlin. They cannot make love to a girl without becoming sentimental. Had Nadya slept with Mario, there might have been the same problem, but the issues would be quite clear. He would be thinking calmly of her money. But with men like Devlin it is different. He came obviously of a good family. I suspected that he had money but that he was not a millionaire. Such a man does not marry *for* money, but peculiarly often he does *marry* money. That is to say, while consciously he would prohibit the base thought, the knowledge of a girl's fortune is the oil upon which a profitable sentimentality slides, and the thought that he is marrying money is subtly countered by the knowledge of his own worth, his family, his background, his eligibility. That eligibility, however – I mean Devlin's eligibility – while it might seem an important factor to the spinsters in Boston, was merely funny in relation to the Pamandari Empire. For I had discovered that the Pamandari wealth was legendary, and the fortune fabulous even in terms of India. The match, therefore, was quite impossible. I would have to take measures to prevent it.

When I went on deck, the conspirators were already together, leaning over the guardrail in approximately the same position as Mario and I had occupied the previous night. When I approached,

I could sense the coolness in Devlin's manner. They had evidently been discussing me. Things were moving quickly. Needless to say, I was angry about the whole thing. In the first place I was not accustomed to having men act coolly towards me, and, secondly, I had looked forward to a long and pleasant trip with Nadya. The trip was now in danger of ending before it had begun. I spoke briefly and inconsequentially to them and then went in search of Mario.

By this time, I had decided that I needed an ally. I could think of no one more qualified to aid me in this piece of intrigue than my lover of the previous night. I found him in the centre of a group of young American women at the swimming pool. At a glance from me, he detached himself from the group and came over. 'I must talk to you at once,' I said.

He said he would meet me in the bar in five minutes.

'The trouble with a man of Devlin's type,' Mario said smoothly, 'is that he has an obstinate conviction of his own worth. All problems must be solved in relation to that conviction. Now, if you were dealing with a man like myself, the problem would be quite different. I, Mario Vassari Ratsonli, Hereditary Duke of Veraggio, with more blue blood in my little finger than that ape has in his whole body, am as poor as a church mouse. If I were the offender, you would only have to say: "Look here, you Hereditary Duke of Veraggio, Mario Vassari Ratsonli, this match is ridiculous. Here are twenty thousand dollars. Now take yourself off like a good boy and let's hear no more of it.' *Et voilà!* I am gone. But with a Bostonian of Devlin's type, the aristocratic tiara is too new and of too doubtful an origin for him to come down off his high horse quickly. For, being essentially a democratic aristocrat, a queer fish altogether, he might find it impossible to remount his horse again! Unlike mine, his title to aristocracy ends when his honour is compromised – ha ha! This is indeed a queer type of aristocracy! But we must treat it seriously, yes, or the consequences may be very serious.'

'What do you suggest?'

'Is the girl in love?'

'She's got hot pants, if that's what you mean.'

'And of course it's very romantic! But her position is from our point of view both advantageous and disadvantageous. This is what I mean. She is spoiled, romantic, and obvious, but it is my guess that she has, unlike him, not a moral fibre in her body, yes?'

'Correct.'

'Very well. Then, in that case she would not listen to a word against him. She would be very obstinate in her defence of him. But, having no morals, she is very vulnerable in another way.'

'What do you mean?'

'I mean that I might be able to seduce her.'

'What good will that do?'

'Ha! There you have it! Perhaps, if there were only her to consider, no good at all. But do you not see that it would be the end as far as Devlin was concerned? It would touch his honour. He would think no more of marriage. If he were I, yes, it would make no difference; he would be after the money. But as that is only, shall we say, an 'afterthought' with him, it would be the end. He would never marry a nymphomaniac.'

'And that's precisely what she is.'

'Of course, and we have only to prove it to him!'

'Do you think you can manage it?'

He hesitated. 'It would mean, I fear, cutting myself off entirely from your society for the rest of the trip.'

'Well, that's alright.'

'Ah, but it would be very painful for me!'

'I will write you a cheque for the equivalent of two thousand dollars if you succeed.'

'Three thousand,' he said quickly. 'There will be certain little expenses . . .'

We agreed upon it. As he kissed my hand, I said, 'And don't try anything with her yourself.' He smiled charmingly:

'You can trust me,' he said. 'I'm a venal man.'

By the time we had passed through the Suez Canal, Nadya and Harry Devlin were no longer on speaking terms. Mario had accomplished his task efficiently and with little apparent effort.

It was about this time that Devlin began to show signs of having an interest in me. The poor young man seemed to be determined to fall in love. I found him handsome enough but wished to keep him as far as possible out of Nadya's sight. I felt that if she could be alone with him for half an hour he might swallow his pride and make a nuisance of himself again.

Meeting Mario on deck one day, he took me aside. He had some information for me, he said. We went to the bar and took a seat in the corner. There, over a drink, he explained to me that, although Nadya was sleeping with him, she had confessed to him that she was still in love with Devlin and had asked him to help her to win him back. This information determined my course of action. I would have to ensnare Devlin myself. We had already rounded the heel of Italy and were making for Marseilles, where Nadya and I were scheduled to disembark and catch the train for Paris. Devlin, as it happened, was catching the same train. As I knew from my own experience, anything might happen during a corridor meeting.

I explained my plan to Mario. It required him to travel to Paris with Nadya and remain there for at least three weeks. He was to see to it that Nadya didn't form any new and equally ridiculous attachments. In return, I offered to pay him seven hundred dollars a week plus expenses. I, meanwhile, would elope with Devlin, carry him off to somewhere on the French Riviera, and join Mario and Nadya in Paris as soon as possible. Mario was delighted with the idea. He had begun to realise that I held the purse-strings of Nadya's entourage, and without being immodest, I believe he was looking forward to the day when we could take up intimacy again at the point at which we had left off. Nadya's childishness had begun to bore him. Once again we parted and once again he assured me in a charming voice that I could have confidence in his venal nature. As we walked round a deserted part of the deck, he took me in his arms, kissed me on the lips, and said: 'Don't be long, Helen.'

I returned immediately to our suite, where I sat down and wrote a long letter to Mr Pamandari. I described in detail the events of the voyage, the reason for the apparent desertion which would take place at Marseilles. I ended saying that I hoped to join Nadya within three weeks at Paris and that meanwhile I felt that Mario, a kind of male counterpart of myself, could be trusted *as long as he was paid* to look after his daughter's interests. If, however, something prevented me from telegramming him within three weeks, Mr Pamandari should himself look into matters as they concerned his daughter. I signed the letter affectionately and posted it at the ship's post office.

Chapter Ten

We were separated yesterday evening. Veiled, I was led out across the courtyard between walls ringing with the white sun and transported in a closed donkey cart across the town. I saw little of it and cannot even guess at the size of it. The building into which I was led is located somewhere near the market. Men and donkeys loaded with fruits were turning a corner nearby and from that direction came the usual market sounds, the guttural voices, an occasional shout and the cries of whipped beasts. Up a flight of wooden stairs, through a door, and into a long passage. They left me in this room at the end of the corridor. The shadows grew longer towards evening. From the slit window I could see the last reflection of the sun on the uneven planes of the roofs. The strains of pipe and zither music rose from somewhere below. A muezzin was crying in a weird singing voice from a minaret. It soon became dark in the room.

The bed is comfortable, broad enough for two.

A short while afterwards a fat Arab woman entered. She grinned at me. Her teeth protruded slightly and she had one gold one. She carried a small oil lamp which she left on the table. She handed a small bowl to me. It contained a mixture which seemed to be of crushed almonds and honey. 'Gut!' she said in pidgin English, rolling her eyes and rubbing her fat paunch with the flat of her hand. I tasted the mixture. It was very pleasant, slightly gritty, and seemed to cause my mouth to tingle slightly. 'Gut!' she repeated with a broad smile. Evidently she was going to remain there until I had finished it. I did so, but quite slowly, partly because the mixture was so sweet and partly because with each successive swallow my stomach tightened, again not unpleasantly, but I found myself breathing more heavily. As I finished the mess in the bowl I lay back on the bed and closed my eyes. Some unknown force seemed to have taken control of my body. I could feel the blood push its way through my veins, my heart seemed to be pounding, and I was involved deliciously and completely in a hypersensitive world of feeling. 'Gut?' she said. I nodded vaguely and she went out.

After she had gone I realised that I had been drugged. My body attained a terrible immediacy of consciousness. If I touched my thigh, it quivered and prickled. I had an urge to bare my belly and watch it rise and fall beyond all knowledge of breathing. The very atmosphere seemed to have weight. It lay on my sensitized skin like an invisible hand. My temples were throbbing. A vast expansion was taking place inside me. I tore off my clothes and lay naked on the bed. In the vast eddying whirlpool of my sensations I lost all consciousness of time. My very breathing afforded me a sexual pleasure. When I touched my mound with my fingertips the acuteness of my pleasure almost caused a spasm, or rather, the sensation was as deliriously brittle as an ordinary spasm, but below, suppurating like a vast nuclear potential, the actual spasm lay in wait, willing blindly to be stimulated. On the other hand, my mind appeared to be unaffected. I saw clearly that I had been drugged for one purpose. For this reason I fought and quenched the desire to precipitate the spasm myself. Instead, I contented myself with brushing the skin of my belly and thighs with my fingertips, and felt my buttocks heave and thrill with an almost unbearably ecstatic sensation. Soon I gave way to an urge towards unconsciousness and seemed to hang impotently between two worlds, heedless of direction. A prickling seizure mounted in the extremities of my limbs, rising gradually and deliriously through every fleshy drain till it lay like steel bands of paralysis at my thighs and armpits. I found myself unable to move a muscle, my consciousness wheeling farther and farther backwards towards utter extinction. At the same time, by thinking casually of my genitals, I hung ecstatically in the balance, a knife of pleasure to its hilt in my sex. This led to the realisation that my throat muscles were not constricted and I uttered a hoarse sob of lust. My eyelids were tightly closed, leadweight, and I lacked the strength to open them. I became, except for the palest eidolon of consciousness, a seamy and pullulating furrow, dark and warm as earth awaiting the sprinkle of seed. Vaguely, through the misted vision of this hothouse paralysis, I heard the door open. A bearded man was bending over me.

As he lowered his naked front on top of me, my bodily reactions were beyond my control. I had the sensation of being a voracious gullet which had been starved for a score of centuries. As his dark member entered me every hair on my bristling body partook of the pleasure. It is impossible to express in any word known to man the impossible peak of pleasure to which his sex transported me. On one level, my vital juices rose up within my belly like the waters of a dam of infinite capacity. I thought it would never end. Literally, no matter how high the waters rose, the limiting walls of potentiality towered massively above. On another level, I experienced a thousand spasms each minute at every pore. On a third and more dispassionate level I was conscious at every moment of the marvellous soft texture of his skin, of the fibrous strength of his short hairs, and of the voluptuous putty-like quality of his tongue. Towards the end, however, I passed out of personality entirely. I became a vessel which threatened and willed at any moment to burst. That burst, when it finally did come, was the most excruciating thing I have ever experienced. If giving birth were pleasant – perhaps it could be – I would compare it to that. The excessive difficulty of the orgasm, the final frantic lurch of the hips in their ecstasy – these things are beyond description. The sting of the reality cannot be contained in words. What, under normal circumstances can be compared with an extremely pleasurable shifting of sands in the womb, became, for a seemingly endless space of time, a vast broiling cauldron of shooting planets. The universe itself suffered annihilation within my womb, and when my limbs, their soft surfaces, swung back into consciousness it was in the sureness and certainty of an utter and oblivious peace.

The man, whoever he was, left as silently as he had come. I lay alone, sweating profusely, and too contented to move. Some time later, another man came. The vast convulsion began all over again. And again, for I counted six others before dawn broke out like a disease on the epidermis of the sky.

It is after noon. I have struggled hard to write what I have written. It seems rather pointless now. But I am so near the end of my story, so near the point at which my leaving Marseilles merges with my present life, that it would be a pity not to go on.

I was fed a short while ago. The same fat woman. The food more succulent than that which I have been used to. Stewed lamb and eggplants. Some kind of rich honeyed pastry afterwards. I rubbed my stomach as the woman did last night, made motions of eating from the small bowl, and said: 'Gut!' questioningly. She laughed with her broad mouth, smacked her large belly, and nodded comprehendingly and said, 'Ya ya ya ya ya ya!' over and over again. I am sure she means I will have more of the mixture tonight. And so meanwhile I shall go on with my story.

But it is difficult to concentrate. My imagination is held by her broad friendly mouth saying, 'Ya ya ya ya ya ya!'

Devlin sat facing me. The train had just pulled out of Toulon on its way to that string of pleasure-spots which constitutes the French Riviera: St Tropez, St Raphael, Cannes, Juan les Pins, Antibes, Nice, and so on to Monte Carlo. We had taken tickets as far as Ventimiglia because in the haste of our departure we had been unable to decide the exact location of our 'honeymoon.' We had eloped. Pretending to have business to do in Marseilles, we had left Nadya in Mario's company, secured our suitcases, and boarded the first train of the Côte d'Azur.

Devlin was in high spirits. We were both, I believe, almost as excited as newlyweds. We had never slept together, and this was in fact a kind of honeymoon. The excitement was heightened by the fact that we had as yet not decided upon our destination, and, as we left each station behind us, unable at the last moment to make up our minds to get off, we experienced a feeling of loss almost, for perhaps we should have got off at St Tropez, or at Cannes, or at Antibes. How were we to know? By the time we reached Nice, we were both feeling a little desperate, but neither one of us was willing to make the necessary decision to get off. Thus we found ourselves running along the coast past Villefranche, St Jean Cap Ferrat, Eze, Cap d'Ail in the direction of Monaco. At Monaco station, Devlin finally took action.

'Let's get the bags,' he said. 'We'll get off at Monte Carlo. It's about two minutes. If we don't, we'll find ourselves in Italy!'

Laughing, I helped him down with the bags, and a few minutes later, the porters were bundling our luggage onto a taxi.

We took rooms at the Hotel de P . . . , bathed, and walked out of the luxurious foyer onto the square.

'That's the Casino,' Devlin said, pointing to the Christmas

cake-like structure that obscured our view of the sea. 'Gambling is one of my vices. We'll go there this evening. Later, we'll go to the Sporting Club, it's a bit more chic. The old Casino's become rather a barn since the First World War.'

Devlin was a mine of information, and his happy and very shy American manner endeared him to me.

I thought little of the fact that our presence here was part of a complicated plan to protect Nadya from him. I accepted the present moment and luxuriated in it. We were sitting on the terrace of the pleasant café that looks onto the Casino square gardens.

'Fabulous things have happened in that Casino,' he said, shaking his head.

'Tell me some of them!'

'Did you never hear the story of the Russian admiral?'

I shook my head.

'I'm not sure when it was,' he said. 'Sometime before the First World War. Part of the Russian Fleet, a couple of heavy cruisers and things were lying offshore. The Admiral came ashore one night and lost a fortune, literally a fortune at the wheels. He returned to his ship in a helluva stew.' At this point Devlin ordered two *fines à l'eau* from the waiter. 'Anyway,' he continued, 'the Admiral returned the next night with the entire payroll of the Russian Fleet. As was to be expected, he lost every penny. He was a broken man. He went to see the boss, whoever he was, and explained to him that he had not only lost his personal fortune, but his honour. He would face a court martial on his return to Russia. He pleaded with this guy to return at least the money which belonged to the Russian Navy. The Casino official was polite but firm. In the way these men have, he explained that if the Admiral had won, the Casino would not have expected reimbursement. The Admiral had to admit that and was persuaded to return to his ship. That might have been the end of the story, but it wasn't. About eleven o'clock in the morning, the Admiral's barge entered the harbour. He took a coach up to the Casino and asked to see the boss again. The boss was none too pleased to see him but the Admiral appeared to be in a very good humour, so he offered him a drink and conducted him into a private room. He asked him what he could do for him. The Admiral explained again that he wanted his money back, only he wanted it all back and not only the money that belonged to the Navy. Of course the official turned nasty. But the Admiral interrupted him. Did the official realise that he (the Admiral) would have to commit suicide? The official said that he was sorry and all that but that there was nothing he could do. The Admiral just smiled. He told the official that the money had better be produced immediately because he had left orders with the fleet that it was to open fire and destroy every stick and stone of Monaco if he had not returned to the flagship by noon. And if he returned without the money he would give the order to open fire himself. It was all the same to him, he explained. If he had to die, he might as well have this little bit of revenge! It was a quarter past eleven. At a quarter to twelve the Admiral's barge returned to the flagship with all the money on board. At twelve-thirty the Russian Fleet steamed away on its Mediterranean cruise!'

Devlin told me of this and many other legends, of the lost fortunes and of the suicides. 'There's a regular graveyard of suicides here,' he said with a laugh.

Later in the afternoon we visited the tropical aquarium, the gardens, drove around the town in an open carriage, did, in fact, all the things which a young honeymoon couple would have done, dined well at our own hotel and ended the evening at the Casino, where Devlin lost a few hundred dollars at roulette.

That night, slightly tipsy and inspired by all the silly things we had done during the day, we lay naked in one another's arms, like a pair of newlyweds, sleeping only when the first light broke through our window.

Looking back, that was the only entirely happy day we spent in each other's company.

As the days passed Devlin drank more and more. He had been losing heavily at the Casino. On the third night he lost $25,000. He kept repeating that it wasn't serious, that he could afford it, but he drank more and by the end of the first week he was going to the Casino at ten o'clock in the morning when it opened. Several times, I tried to get him to cut his losses, but he grew more and more bad-tempered and began to blame me for ill-luck.

'If you don't want to come with me, then for God's sake stay in the hotel! Do you think a man can gamble when there's someone looking over his shoulder watching every move he makes? Stay in the hotel, goddamn you, and leave me alone!'

I did so for two nights, but he lost more heavily than ever, returning completely drunk to our room in the early hours of the morning. I tried to encourage him to leave Monte Carlo.

The third night we went out together. We walked silently upwards away from the Casino. He had obviously no wish to go there with me. And yet I felt he was quite glad to have my company.

I had a sudden brainwave.

'Let's drive to Nice tonight,' I said. 'It'll do you good to get away from here for a few hours.'

He was immediately eager.

'We'll hire a car,' he said.

It was still light. We drove along the Moyenne Corniche with the Mediterranean down below us to the left, exposed suddenly between rocks and villas, glimmering blue-grey patches of darkening sea. Devlin was driving and he didn't speak much. He pointed out an occasional villa whose owner he knew or had read about.

'Some people live here all the year round,' he said, 'but that type usually hasn't much money. Nice is different. It's also a city.'

We descended at last, ran quickly through Nice to the sea front, and drove slowly along the Promenade des Anglais. We came to a halt opposite a side street whose discreet neon bar signs stretched backwards in the near darkness towards the old city.

'A drink?'

I nodded. 'Park the car, anyway,' I said.

A moment later we entered a softly lighted bar and sat in one corner at the back.

Three single women were sitting at the bar. They were dressed rather daringly in unfashionable evening dresses, cut low to expose a naked expanse of back. Their legs, their heavy thighs smooth under silk, dangled indolently from high stools. They glanced at us occasionally. Two of them were not remarkable in any way, women merely, like taxis waiting, over a small drink, for whatever men might enter. But the third, though obviously a prostitute also, was different. Her curves were softer than those of the other two, who were almost hard in their angularity. She had richly flowing black hair which sprouted out of a low and startlingly white forehead. Her fleshy face, with its big lips and high cheekbones, was, I felt, softly desirable, as the warm breadth of her hips certainly was, and the heavy but well-shaped flesh of her arms. Devlin, I could see, was obviously attracted by her. She glanced at us more than the other two, almost inviting us to call her over.

'What about it?' I said to Devlin with a smile.

He pretended not to understand.

'What about what?' he said.

'That woman,' I said. 'We could take her to a hotel.'

He flushed. 'We?'

'Of course,' I said. 'You don't expect me to wait for you, do you?'

'Who said anything about her?' Devlin said.

'Don't be silly! You're dying to take her to bed with you!'

Devlin laughed. 'I think you're exaggerating!'

'Well, you'd like to anyway.' As he didn't deny it, I went on. 'And she's just the right build. She'd make love very smoothly. It'd be a pleasure to watch her.'

'Now we're getting at the truth,' Devlin said with a smile.

'Let's call her over.'

'You're sure?'

'Of course I am,' I said.

I watched Devlin make what was meant to be a discreet but what turned out to be a very obvious gesture.

Smiling, the woman slipped down off the stool and approached us with a voluptuous walk. The other two looked at us almost with contempt, but I held their eyes and theirs were lowered first.

'Hillo! You want something?' said the big girl who confronted us.

'Won't you join us in a drink?' Devlin said with his most attractive smile.

'I like to very much,' the woman replied.

Devlin seated her and called the waiter. The woman wanted whisky and soda. It was brought to her.

'You are on holiday?'

'We're on our honeymoon,' I said with a smile.

The woman didn't seem the least put out.

'I have many friends on their honeymoon,' she said ambiguously, for she didn't speak much English.

'In that case you will know roughly what we want,' I said suggestively.

'Roughly? I don't undersatained roughly . . .' said the woman, somewhat nervously.

Devlin laughed. '*C'est-à-dire, rien,*' he said in his best French. '*Rien? Comment rien?*'

Devlin waved his hand in the air as though to erase what had been said.

'*Elle vous a demandé,*' he said slowly, '*si vous savez faire comme il faut.*' He ended his sentence with a vague motion of the hand.

'*Moi!*' said the big girl with a broad smile, '*mais bien sûr!*'

'Because if you don't,' I said with a smile, 'you're going to learn!'

'Ah weee!' said the girl, 'I teach you. No worry!'

We were all smiling at one another. The girl said to Devlin: 'She is vairy beautiful, you wife.'

'But he's going to enjoy you all the same,' I said.

'Aren't you, Harry?'

'What she say?' said the girl.

'*Elle a dit que tu es belle aussi,*' Devlin said.

'*Ah oui, moi!*' said the girl bursting into laughter.

'Look at all that flesh, Harry,' I said cruelly. 'Aren't you just dying to knead it in your hands?'

'It was your idea,' he said, somewhat hurt.

I laughed. 'Yes, I know it was, darling. I'm just dying to see you mount her!'

'I'm not so sure it's a good idea,' he said pompously.

'What he say?' the girl said.

'He says it's time we started,' I said.

'Good,' the girl said. 'I got hotel. You come with me.'

Harry paid up silently and followed us out.

'I do for mainy honeymoons copples,' said the girl as we walked through the revolving door into the street. 'They all have very good time!'

I put my arm round her waist. 'I'm sure they do,' I said.

Harry followed a few paces behind, like a scolded dog.

I watched the girl's superb buttocks mount the narrow stair in front of me, glossy and full of promise as ripe melons, and I imagined her then and there opening her thighs for a man, and, like a ripe melon from which a large slice had been extracted, she was at that part hung with a wet and ambiguous core, her clung seam voracious between her widening knees. And there indeed she was after a few moments, after she had taken Devlin into the *cabinet*, and returned in her various body garters to set herself like a goblet of lust on the bed. She was fatter, the flesh thicker, than I had expected.

A moment later, Devlin came through from the *cabinet*. He was naked except for his socks and obviously embarrassed.

'Come make me warm!' the girl said. 'Your wife watch just now.'

With a last glance, almost of hatred, towards me, Devlin laid himself down close to the woman's gleaming chops. When she laughed, the voluptuous heaviness of her belly quivered. She reached out and drew him towards her. His reluctant body arched and then fell passively against her. She wrapped him in her folds and with softly muttered words inspired a slight rotatory movement at his hips. She grunted as though with pleasure, allowed her thick dark head to fall backwards onto the pillow, and, cupping him in her hands at the buttocks, urged him forwards towards his passion. Then she allowed her head to roll sideways like a doll's, his face buried in her neck, and she looked up at me and said throatily: 'It wonderful!'

I smiled. The woman was obviously bored. But that, after all, was what she was paid for. I moved forward and knelt beside the bed, watching closely as in the increasing wetness the hairs of his belly combed hers, voluptuously with a ripple at the meeting of muscles. I couldn't resist what I did next. I slid one hand in between the oiled heat of their bodies, searching between two glowering brows of hair for the rising masticity, and found it, with the delicate hooks of my fingers, pleasant to stimulate, the woman breathing harder under my experienced touch, and the flat bounding wall of my lover almost frantic now to bring about its assertion.

But how for me?

Swiftly, I removed all my clothes and threw myself naked beside them. I had to prise my knee between them to separate them, my thigh as it moved between the slickness of their sweat wedging them apart. I was concerned now only with my own urgency. But I had counted without the strength of Devlin's desire. He was beyond thought. His one desire was to be sucked right into the pit of his bought woman. He had no time for me. He grasped me at the knee and prised my leg outwards again, causing his belly to meet again in a hot flap with the dark girl's. Her thighs were now working like pistons.

I struck backwards, wet a towel under the tap, and, using it as a whip, I struck the pair again as they rolled about the bed. But my blows only made them more passionate and finally, in disgust, I hurled the towel aside. At that moment, his whole frame quivering, Devlin uttered a groan of fulfilment. The prostitute, with the slickness of an electric light switch, became business-like. She slipped from underneath him, and, grinning at me, walked over towards the *cabinet*. Devlin lay with his face buried in the pillow.

'What about me?' I said angrily.

He didn't answer. I crossed to the door and threw it open. As it happened, coming down the stairs was a Negro soldier. When he saw me naked at the door he stopped and grinned. I beckoned to him to follow me. I lay down on the other bed and opened my arms to the unknown man. He took in the situation at a glance, grinned, and, a moment later, was at me with his hard core. All the while as I groaned with passion and pleasure. Devlin watched, his head on one cheek on the pillow, but his obvious horror only acted as a catalyst to my delicate lust. And, a few moments later, when the prostitute returned fully dressed, I felt the delicious shift at my vital centre and I slid softly like a tadpole's moving into my delirium.

As I returned to my senses, the woman was hooting with laughter, and Devlin, already dressed, was disappearing through the doorway. What a bore! I remember thinking. By the time I had extricated myself from the clutches of my Negro lover, Devlin was completely gone, that's to say the car was missing from the place we had parked it.

More bored than angry, I returned to Monte Carlo by taxi.

We made it up the following day, but he was already back in the clutches of his gambling mania. Things had gone too far.

'I'll try once more, Helen. I promise, that'll be the last time. Only you come with me tonight.'

I agreed, happy that he seemed to be coming to his senses. We arrived in the Casino after dinner towards ten o'clock at night. He wrote a cheque for $1,000 and began to play roulette. I watched him play an indecisive game for some time, winning and losing, winning and losing, being slightly down after the first half hour. I noticed that many of the habitués, that breed of human being which lingers on at Monte Carlo, having come there and lost everything or almost everything before 1914, the person who bets approximately the same number of francs as he did half a century ago and pretends not to notice that the currency has depreciated. They took a vicarious pleasure in watching the undulations of Devlin's fortune, sharing his small triumphs and sneakingly triumphant at his sudden misfortunes. Old gentlemen with white hair, clad dapperly in moth-eaten black suits, old women in unfashionable evening dresses, supporting gaudy strings of artificial pearls, and fixing a tense face, built up of layers of powder and rouge, on the spinning wheel. I suppose they recognised in Devlin a compatriot, that is to say 'a born loser,' a man who is going to win, but always tomorrow, and were fascinated by the familiar ritual of a man on his way to destitution. I thought I glimpsed a certain sadness, a certain reluctance to take this young man's money, in the eyes of the croupiers. As he became more reckless – they had watched him now for over a week – their faces assumed a wooden unexpressiveness. As I turned away to go to the bar, I caught the eye of an old lady who was sniffing eau de cologne in her handkerchief. Her eyes left the ambiguous blur of the spinning wheel, and as she looked at me almost – I felt it with a shiver – with a gleam of lust in her watery eyes, her bird's head seemed to nod in a kind of occult sympathy with the clock-clock-clock-clock of the settling ball.

I walked quickly away in the direction of the bar.

In my haste, I walked at full tilt into a young man in a white dinner jacket. He apologised profusely and I found him leading me into the bar.

Over our drinks he introduced himself as Youssef . . .*. He was some kind of sheikh. His yacht, he said, was in the bay. At any other time I would have been fascinated by the dark good looks of this young Arab, but at that moment, I could think of little else but of Devlin's madness. Ten minutes later, out of the corner of my eyes, I saw my lover pass across the floor

---

* The family name of this personage has been suppressed for official reasons.

of the next room and return a moment later with hands and pockets stuffed with large chips. He had obviously been to cash another cheque.

'The young American,' Youssef said, 'you are his friend?'

I nodded.

'It is a great pity,' he said, shaking his head. 'I have watched him now for over a week. He has lost a small fortune.'

'Do you play yourself?'

'Sometimes, when I feel I'm on a lucky streak. I actually win. But it takes a certain amount of discipline.'

I didn't reply.

'Have another drink,' he said kindly. 'It will make you feel better. He is not your husband?'

'No.'

'I'm glad of that, for there is little you can do.'

'About his gambling?'

He nodded.

About midnight, Devlin lurched into the bar. He was as pale as a ghost. He glanced for a moment at us and then strode over to the bar. He drank a number of brandies one after the other. I made to get up and go over to him but Youssef restrained me.

'It's better not,' he said. 'He'll come when he's ready.'

Five minutes later Devlin came.

He looked at the Arab with something approaching a look of hate.

'Are you with him or with me?' he snapped.

Youssef stood up apologetically. 'Please sit down, sir. I was merely keeping the lady company until you returned.'

'Blow, wog!' Devlin said coarsely.

'Harry!'

'And you shut your damn little mouth!'

Youssef was staring dangerously at Devlin's drunken face.

'I thought I told you to blow?'

'I will leave in my own good time,' the Arab said with an effort. 'To lose is stupid, but to lose badly is disgusting.'

'Oh, you think so, do you?' Devlin leered. 'Well, I'll let you into a little secret. Your opinion doesn't concern me, wog! Savvy? Speakada Inglees?'

The sheikh controlled himself. 'If you hadn't already lost your fortune as well as your manners,' he began . . .

Devlin laughed hoarsely. 'What do you know about it? You want to play for high stakes, you perfumed camel man?'

'Don't play with him, Youssef!' I cried.

'Don't play with him!' mimicked Devlin, and then he turned to me. 'You keep out of this, you bitch! Just . . . keep . . . your . . . trap . . . shut!'

'I believe we are staying at the same hotel,' Youssef said calmly. 'My suite is on the first floor.' He turned to me, 'Goodnight, mademoiselle.'

'If you go to his rooms, I shall leave you,' I said after the sheikh had gone.

'What was the proverb about the rats?' Devlin asked into the air as he made his way over to the bar for another drink.

3 a.m. I sat up late in our room, waiting for Devlin to return. For the first time in my life I was certain, absolutely certain, of my own motives. I wanted to leave him because I disliked him. I found it difficult to forgive his coarse insults. At the same time, his remark about the rats affected me deeply. It was true that he had lost a great deal of money, more than he could afford, and now I was quite certain that he was on the first floor in Youssef's suite. If I was any judge of character, it would be Devlin who would

lose. It was this reluctance to desert him when he was down that caused me to await his return. I had smoked almost a packet of cigarettes since returning to the room.

When he came in, he was paler than before but apparently sober. He flopped down on an armchair without a word and stared at the carpet. I fixed him a drink and carried it across to him. He took it quietly. A moment later he said:

'I'm finished, Helen.'

His voice sounded so small and pathetic that I ran over to his side and sat on the floor beside his chair. He ran his fingers through my hair.

'I've written cheques for over $100,000 at the Casino,' he said slowly. 'And as for that damn Arab, he has my notes for more than $120,000. God knows whether I've got that amount of money in the world!'

'Oh, Harry! Look, darling. I'll tell you what I'll do. I'll speak to Youssef. I'll get him to give you your notes back.'

'You'll do no such thing! I'd rather die.'

'Don't be a fool, Harry!'

'Good God, do you think I could let you do that after the way I insulted him?'

'You could apologise.'

'To *him*!'

'I think you're being foolish, Harry.'

'You want me to go creeping on my knees to him?'

'If necessary, *yes*!'

'You'll wait a long time and more for *that*!'

'I don't think it would be necessary. I'm sure he would give the notes to me.'

'I'll see him in hell first!'

I shrugged hopelessly, walked across to the mantelpiece, and lit a cigarette.

'What do you intend to do?'

'I've been thinking, Helen,' he said eagerly.

'It's about time,' I answered drily.

'Don't be like that, Helen! What's done's done. As for the future, that all depends on you.'

'How?'

'I shall have to go back to the States and get a job.'

'Well?'

'I want you to come with me,' he said eagerly.

'We'll be poor for a while but we'll make out somehow. If only you'll come with me . . .'

'That's out of the question.' I tried to say it as gently as possible but he looked as though I had struck him on the face.

'What do you mean "out of the question"?'

'Just that, Harry. I won't go with you.'

'Am I so repulsive all of a sudden?' he sneered.

'You're not repulsive at all, at least not now you aren't. The point is that I'm not in love with you and, anyway, I wouldn't make a good poor man's wife.'

'So you're going to walk out on me?'

'That's hardly a fair way to put it. I'll do as much as I can. I'll stay with you for a few weeks if it will help. I could let you have a few thousand dollars.'

'Conscience money!'

'You've no right to talk that way, Harry! You brought it all on yourself.' I had been about to say, 'You've had your fling,' but I didn't have the heart to.

'Are you walking out on me or aren't you?'

'I've already answered that question.'

'Very well,' he said bitterly. He was looking pale and drawn. He got up and walked through into the other bedroom. I sat down unsteadily on the arm of the chair he had vacated. I wasn't feeling altogether hopeless about Devlin's situation because I felt sure that Youssef would return the notes to me. As far as the Casino losses were concerned, there was nothing we could do. Devlin wasn't a Russian Admiral and he had no fleet anchored in the bay. And anyway, perhaps only a Russian could have acted in such a swashbuckling manner.

I stood up. There was no point in wasting time. I would go at once to see Youssef. Devlin would undoubtedly feel better when he had cut his losses by more than half. But as I walked towards the door a loud explosion took place in the next room. I froze momentarily and then, with a wild cry, threw myself towards the bedroom.

Horrified, I was standing staring at the corpse which a few minutes ago had been a live and passionate man. I was shivering with terror, rooted to the spot, when I felt a hand take me at the elbow. It was Youssef.

'The young fool!' he said, looking down at the lifeless body. 'I was just on my way to give him the notes back.'

'It will not be necessary for you to go ashore again,' Youssef said as he approached me along the deck.

Shortly after the suicide, he had spirited me on board his yacht, and I was standing on the quarterdeck looking at the ghostly early morning outline of the prince's castle at Monaco.

'The police are quite satisfied that it is a clear case of suicide. I asked for you to be excused to avoid publicity. They were quite understanding about it.'

I thanked him.

'Why did he do it?' Youssef said suddenly.

'What do you mean?'

He laughed nervously. 'I mean, did he say anything to you? Give you any indication?'

'None whatsoever. I told him I wouldn't marry him and he got angry and said I was running out on him.'

'Were you?'

'It was hardly like that. I offered to stay with him for a while.'

'But he must obviously have blamed you for his suicide, I mean he did it to impress you.'

'I don't see how you can say that! I wouldn't marry him and go and live in America with him. But surely that was no reason for him to go and shoot himself.'

'I think it probably was his reason.'

'And what about you! It was you who ruined him!'

'We were both to blame, perhaps,' Youssef said gently.

'Or neither of us. He was mad. I told him you would give him his notes back. I was just coming to you when I heard the shot.'

'A postmortem won't help anyway,' Youssef said. 'Look, Helen, we're both of us upset about this. Why don't we get out of here, now, this minute. A couple of weeks holiday would do you the world of good.'

'Where?'

'North Africa,' he said. 'We can make for Algiers.'

'For two weeks?'

'As long as you care to come for,' he said, looking into my eyes.

'Yes, I think I'd like that,' I said finally.

Half an hour later the sleek white yacht slipped quietly out of the harbour into the Mediterranean.

Chapter Eleven

I have not added anything to my account for over a week. I have seldom been able to isolate the desire. It has existed as the consciousness of something left undone in the kaleidoscopic matrix of my feelings, like a patch, an imperfection on a quilt, which, with the passage of time, comes to blend with the material of the quilt until in the end, except to close scrutiny, it is imperceptible.

God knows my original desire was strong enough. I felt I must put into words the teeming mass of experience I have lived through. At the beginning, there was a distinct desire for revenge against Youssef, who, to resolve the guilt on his own conscience, thrust my present life upon me. Intellectually, that desire still exists, but it is a mere shadow, bloodless, like a textbook recommendation. And gradually the whole desire to commit my experiences to history has been outflanked by the terrible pleasure I experience in approaching the unconscious state of an object, an amorphous mass of sensitive flesh and fibre without the form of will. It is indeed doubtful whether I can still usefully use the word 'I.' Certainly the governing vision that in the past I used to identify with myself has grown so dim during most of my 'waking' hours as not to be a personality at all. I have lusted as it were to melt out of myself, to become the anonymous and vibrant plasm which the regular application of drugs – hashish I believe – has made me. I am indescribably lazy. Breathing itself is such a pleasant effort! The vague and exciting apprehension of the nights when my unknown lovers will visit me, ramming their hard and lustful bodies against the soft willingness which is my shuddering flesh, that apprehension is for the most part the only 'thought' which occupies my consciousness. And even that – I have only to close my eyes and sigh to experience an ecstatic tumescence at the core of my belly and to send minute ripples of tingling pleasures across the broad plains of my peerless skin.

I am Narcissus. I look into the water and find myself beautiful, indeed, the only beauty. The comings and goings of my 'lovers' are merely the gentle showers which nurture the plant. And the plant is myself, living on and on with a slow stirring motion through nights and days and nights and days of voluptuousness.

What an effort it is to write this! I yawn. I clap my hand to that vast bud of sex which is strapped like a sweetly odoriferous gully between my mountainous thighs. I experience an earthquake. I laugh a deep laugh of mammal content, a laugh which I do not recognise as the superficial titter which in the past was evoked by an amusing situation. No. This is the laugh of flesh which has inherited the earth. Oh God, what an ecstasy!

Food? Its taste is very pleasant, but it is rather an effort to eat it. All I eat willingly and without reservation is the exotic mouth-ringing mixture of honey and almonds and . . .

I seem to be getting farther and farther away from the conclusion of my story. I think: 'I must begin now. An hour or two is all that is necessary. Now. Get the paper. See, it is still light outside. See, there is the marketplace over there. In the distance. How bright the colours are in their haze! A heat haze I suppose. And the buildings startlingly white . . .'

But what was I trying to say? The warmth comes up to me from the street. Where am I? I am sitting again on the bed. I am clenching my teeth. I am trying to concentrate. Yes. I am on a yacht . . .

. . . arriving at Algiers.

'You'll love the desert, Helen!' Youssef whispered. His dark handsome face appeared behind me in the mirror, tilted forwards as his lips sought my bare neck.

I had been dressing. I was standing in my panties and my brassiere in front of the long mirror, fastening my long sheer nylon stockings to my garter belt in preparation for going ashore.

'You're keeping me back,' I laughed. 'Why don't you be a good boy and look out of the porthole?'

'When I can look at you?' His soft lips moved deliriously at the soft skin of my shoulder.

'Is that what you call "looking"?'

'Looking, feeling, kissing, loving,' he said, holding me backwards against him so that the firm rounds of my buttocks were warm and close at his groin. 'What a beautiful body you've got, Helen!'

'Thank you, sir. But if you want me to see this beautiful desert of yours you'd better allow me to dress.'

'I don't want you to dress,' he said. 'I'd like you to be naked, always. Naked and hot.'

'I'm always hot. Sometimes it's not possible to be naked.'

He laughed and bit me playfully on the shoulder.

'You're a hot bitch!'

'Hot I certainly am, and bitch I may be, but I don't see the necessity for the conjunction. And now, dear sheikh, please step backwards while I put my skirt on.'

He sat in a chair, watching me dress, and lit a cigarette.

'Will I see a mirage?' I said.

'What do you want with a mirage?'

'Nothing particularly. I was just trying to make pleasant conversation with a native.'

'Bitch!'

'Sheikh!'

'Tart!'

'Camel boy!'

'Oh Helen!' He had stood up again and was now crushing his lips against mine. He moved backwards with me to the bunk, laying the top half of my body on top of it. Then, with his right hand, and with the careless effort of a man who can afford anything, he ripped, literally tore, my web-like panties from off my loins.

'*What* do you think you're doing!' I said playfully.

'I'm going to f – you!'

'Again?'

He answered me in fact, penetrating my warm sheath in the same buccaneering fashion. Our movements were quick and passionate. As his passion rose into me, there was a discreet knock on the door.

'Da . . . amn!' he said breathlessly. 'We've arrived!'

'You have indeed,' I said drily. 'And now would you mind going up on deck while I clean up and get dressed?'

For a reason I didn't understand then, Youssef was unwilling to pass even one night in a hotel in Algiers. We drove straight from the harbour to Blida, where we went to the house of a friend of his. We passed the evening charmingly, listening to singing and watching an extremely sensual Arab dancer.

Next morning, we continued on our journey, the destination of which he refused to disclose to me.

I told him that I didn't have a great deal of time, that I would have to fly to Paris within a week but that I would rejoin him as soon as possible. He was very offhand about it but said that I could get an aeroplane from the interior.

A few days later, we abandoned the car and took to camels. There were probably twenty camels in the train. I found it amusing but rather tiring.

At one point a strange thing happened. I could have sworn I saw another white woman one time when we were camped by an oasis. Youssef laughed and said that I had seen my 'mirage.' I dismissed the incident from my mind immediately. I was content to enjoy my present happiness, the strangely exhilarating quality of the desert, fold upon fold of sand sweeping away to mauve imprecision on the horizon, and the nights on warm rugs in the gaudy tent with my lover, now wearing Arab clothes, and more passionate and lustful than ever. The thought occurred to me occasionally that there might be another white woman in the caravan, but it made no difference to me. Even if she was Youssef's mistress, what did it matter? I don't remember ever being jealous of a man.

It was on the third day that it happened.

Youssef appeared to have obtained a horse from somewhere or other, a large white gelding on which he pranced backwards and forwards the length of the caravan. I asked him if he could get me a horse. 'What for?' he said. His tone was rather contemptuous.

'Because I want one,' I said, an element of indignation in my voice.

'No. It's impossible,' he said quickly.

We stopped early at an oasis that day.

I reopened the subject.

'Why can't you get me a horse? You got one for yourself!'

He looked at me with a cold smile.

'You won't need a horse where you're going,' he said.

'What do you mean by that?'

'You'll soon find out!' he said, and he turned to a group of Arabs who were squatting beside a tree. He shouted something in Arabic to them. Two of them dissociated themselves from the group and came towards us. When they were close, he pointed to me and walked off beyond the trees. I felt my arms pinioned by the two Arabs and we followed in his wake. I was frightened, but I couldn't help feeling that Youssef looked like a circus character with his shining boots and his burnous and the whip he carried in his right hand. He walked a little distance off behind a dune and waited. I was dragged again into his presence.

'What's all this about?' I said angrily as soon as I confronted him.

'Shut your damn mouth!' he said and struck me across the face with the whip.

'You'll be sorry for that,' I said.

He roared with laughter.

'You little fool!' he said. 'Don't you realise that you're in my country? Don't you realise that I can do just what I please with you?'

'You'd better be careful!' I said. I don't know why I said it. I felt angry and powerless and very afraid. I think I must have been thinking vaguely of Mr Pamandari, although what he could do even I failed to see. In fact, he could do nothing.

'You had better forget all that, Helen,' Youssef said more quietly. 'This is the last time I shall see you. I'm going to give myself the pleasure of watching you being raped by these men. After that I'm going to turn you over to them.'

'Why?'

'A favour to a friend,' Youssef said. 'Devlin's brother was a friend of mine. I was educated in America.'

'You damn fool! What has that got to do with me?'

'I really don't know,' he said with a smile which, when it left his lips, was the signal for the two men to throw themselves upon me, rip off my clothes, and rape me there on the sand.

In the flurry of dust and grunts and the frantic flailing of my own outraged limbs, I saw Youssef walk away.

'Youssef!'

But a brown hand was clamped over my mouth and a brutal urgency jabbed at my exposed and twitching loins. I was still lying there and my violators, calmer now, were sitting smoking and watching me, when I saw part of the camel train move off, Youssef on his white horse riding out of sight without once turning his head in my direction.

How I hated that man!

There is nothing more to tell. My hatred lost its edge a long time ago. I have became gradually acclimatized. Willingly. But that does not prevent me, intellectually at least, from despising the man who is responsible for my fate. He knew Devlin's brother! Salved his own conscience by behaving brutally towards me! What a despicable little man! I bear him no malice, but I hope he burns in hell for it!

This writing, what a bore! How gently, how sweetly tired I am! It is growing dark. Soon the muezzin will cry out to bring the faithful to prayer. What a wonderful religion that a woman is allowed to experience so much and so deeply! But there is a canker of hatred for Youssef which I am unable to eradicate. He didn't wish me well though I was a good mistress to him. He thought he was punishing me. I would like to be avenged.

Where is Nadya? Where is Mario? What has Mr Pamandari done about them? The questions lose in definition day by day. The answers become of purely academic interest. I must put this manuscript away. My keeper will be here shortly with my beloved potion. After that I will write no more. One last word.

I am almost sorry it is over. I feel a certain nostalgia. But that is irrelevant. I cannot put my pencil down. I have the urge to write more. And yet the story is ended. I have a vague feeling that I have left a great deal unsaid. But why am I so certain that it should be said at all? There is no reason for anything to be said. Saying is stupid. A ridiculous waste of time that might otherwise be *lived*. I think I write because it is a triumph. I feel the need to express that triumph. Of course it wasn't so at the beginning. Then, I had a reason to write. I vaguely felt, I suppose, that someday this manuscript would lie on a desk behind which a man was sitting. What man? A man, I suppose, who would wish to avenge me. That little piece of dirty business cleaned up and I will be happy. I am happy now. But that righteous fool Youssef! That he should exist is an impertinence. Worse. Sacrilege. What am I doing still wielding this pencil? It seems to have stuck to my fingers. I can't get rid of it. Shores of experience slide away from me. The sky will be red tonight from my slit of a window. The rooftops and the minaret at sunset will glow softly and noises of beasts and men and perhaps music will drift up to me before – after, oh yes, after my beloved potion!—the door opens for another time and with a rising of my juices a male spine drives me to delirium.

I must put . . .

(*End of Manuscript*)

COPY OF A LETTER SENT BY MAJOR PIERRE JAVET TO
HIS FRIEND, CAPTAIN JACQUES DECOEUR OF THE
FRENCH GARRISON AT MASCARA, ALGERIA.

Ghardaïa,
1 October 1949.

Dear Jacques,

*Over two months have passed since that strange manuscript came
into our hands.*

*Extensive investigations have been made, here, in Algiers, and
even in Oran, but little information has come to light.*

*Two Arabs confessed to seeing 'a white woman' in the camel
train of Sheikh X . . . , but when we questioned him about it – he
is an influential man in these parts, so we had to move cautiously
– he said that there was indeed 'a white woman,' a Persian dancer
who is now in his harem. He even produced a photograph of her,
taken, he says, at Blida. Meanwhile, the two witnesses, wily birds
that they are, say that they could not positively identify the woman,
and that the Persian woman may well be the woman they saw. We
checked the story and were able to confirm that this Persian dancer
did actually travel with the caravan. There was no secret about
it. On the contrary, for a woman about to go to a harem, it was
suspiciously well publicised.*

*My own feelings, of course, are that this was 'the white woman'
whom Helen Smith (or Seferis) said she saw. But there it is. We
are at a dead end in our investigations. The woman most certainly
did exist. We have confirmation of that from Australia, Singapore,
India, and Monte Carlo. Whether she still exists, God knows. My
own guess is that she is in some Arab brothel from which it would
be devilishly difficult to extricate her.*

*This might have been all. But Good God, Jacques, we had
reckoned without one of the characters! I didn't give a second
thought to Mr Pamandari – a kindly and rich old Parsee, that
was my impression. And because of Miss Smith's queer attachment
to him, because of the fact that she might have been said to have
been in his employ, I took the liberty of sending a copy of the
manuscript to him. With some misgivings because of the references
to his daughter, Nadya, I admit. I didn't realise precisely what
I was stirring up.*

'In fact, he could do nothing.' *That is what Helen Smith
wrote, if you remember. That, I take it now, is the only untrue
assertion in the whole manuscript.*

*I had no idea who this Mr Pamandari was. A fortnight after I
send the manuscript to him, I received a polite note of thanks in
which he said that he would look into the matter. That was all.*

*But it turned out that although our sheikh was a powerful
man, when compared to the venerable old Mr Pamandari, he
was a minnow beside an octopus. We soldiers sometimes don't
realise what forces go on behind the scenes!*

*To be brief, Mr Pamandari brought pressure to bear on the
Arab League and in the middle of September Sheikh X . . . was
assassinated in Laghouat. Mysteriously, of course, no questions,
no evidence. And now, by God, the whole district is in an uproar!
There is a team of investigators who pooh-pooh our efforts and who
confidently predict that they will discover the whereabouts of the*

unfortunate woman within a month. If and when they do so, God knows what is going to happen, but we have already received a note from the Governor General that all Mr Pamandari's wishes are to be respected to the letter! Et voilà, my boy, that is all I know!

A good-natured member of the Foreign Office who was holidaying here smiled when I mentioned Mr Pamandari. His words were: 'It's no use asking what Mr Pamandari has to do with this or that. He owns it.'

A bientôt.

Pierrot.

Rebel Inc. magazine was started in 1992 by **Kevin Williamson**, with help from established young authors **Duncan McLean** and **Gordon Legge**. It set out with the intention of promoting and publishing what was then seen as a new wave of young urban Scottish writers who were kicking back against the literary mainstream.

The Rebel Inc. imprint is a development of the magazine ethos, publishing accessible as well as challenging texts aimed at extending the domain of counter-culture literature.

Children of Albion Rovers Welsh, Warner, Legge, Meek, Hird, Reekie
£5.99 pbk
"Pacy, punchy, state of the era." *iD*

The Man with the Golden Arm Nelson Algren £7.99 pbk
"This is a man writing and you should not read it if you cannot take a punch ... Mr Algren can hit with both hands and move around and he will kill you if you are not awfully careful ... Mr Algren, boy you are good." **Ernest Hemingway**

Revenge of the Lawn Richard Brautigan £6.99 pbk
"His style and wit transmit so much energy that energy itself becomes the message. Brautigan makes all the senses breathe. Only a hedonist could cram so much life onto a single page." ***Newsweek***

Sombrero Fallout Richard Brautigan £6.99 pbk
"Playful and serious, hilarious and melancholy, profound and absurd ... how delightfully unique a prose writer Brautigan is." ***TLS***

Fup Jim Dodge £7.99 hbk
"An extraordinary little book ... as good as writing gets." ***Literary Review***

Stone Junction Jim Dodge, introduced by Thomas Pynchon £7.99 pbk
"Reading *Stone Junction* is like being at a non-stop party in celebration of everything that matters." **Thomas Pynchon**

The Sinaloa Story Barry Gifford £6.99 pbk
"Gifford cuts through to the heart of what makes a good novel readable and entertaining." **Elmore Leonard**

The Wild Life of Sailor and Lula Barry Gifford £8.99 pbk
"Gifford is all the proof that the world will ever need that a writer who listens with his heart is capable of telling anyone's story." **Armistead Maupin**

The Blind Owl Sadegh Hedayat, introduced by Alan Warner £6.99 pbk
"One of the most extraordinary books I've ever read. Chilling and beautiful."
The Guardian

Nail and Other Stories Laura Hird £8.99 pbk
"Confirms the flowering of a wonderfully versatile imagination on the literary
horizon." *Independent on Sunday*

The Drinkers' Guide to the Middle East Will Lawson £5.99 pbk
"Acerbic and opinionated ... it provides a surprisingly perceptive and practical
guide for travellers who want to live a little without causing a diplomatic incident."
The Guardian

My Brother's Gun Ray Loriga £6.99 pbk
"A fascinating cross between Marguerite Duras and Jim Thompson."
Pedro Almodovar

Kill Kill Faster Faster Joel Rose £6.99 pbk
"A modern urban masterpiece." **Irvine Welsh**

Snowblind Robert Sabbag, introduced by Howard Marks £6.99 pbk
"A flat-out ballbuster. It moves like a threshing machine with a full tank of ether.
This guy Sabbag is a whip-song writer." **Hunter S Thompson**

A Life in Pieces Campbell / Niel, eds £10.99 pbk
"Trocchi's self-fragmented lives and works are graphically recalled in this sensitively
orchestrated miscellany." *The Sunday Times*

Young Adam Alexander Trocchi £6.99 pbk
"Everyone should read *Young Adam*." *TLS*

Helen & Desire Alexander Trocchi £6.99 pbk
"A spicily pornographic tale ... enhanced by an elegant and intelligent introduction
by Edwin Morgan." *The Scotsman*

Drugs and the Party Line Kevin Williamson £5.99 pbk/ £6.99 Hemp pbk
"Essential reading for Blair, his Czar, and the rest of us."
Matthew Collin, *The Face*

Call us for a free **Rebel Inc. sampler**, which gives more information on all the
above titles. The sampler also contains extracts from our most recent publications,
together with information about the authors, tours and competitions.
All of the above titles are available in good bookshops, or can be ordered directly from:
Canongate Books, 14 High Street, Edinburgh EH1 1TE
Tel 0131 557 5111 Fax 0131 557 5211
email info@canongate.co.uk   http://www.canongate.co.uk
All forms of payment are accepted and p&p is free to any address in the UK